MW01144220

BILLIONAIRE'S SECRET ATTRACTION

A BILLIONAIRE ROMANCE

MICHELLE LOVE

CONTENTS

Taken by A Billionaire   vii

1. Caleb   1
2. Caleb   4
3. Madison   8
4. Caleb   11
5. Madison   16
6. Madison   23
7. Caleb   28
   Desired by a Billionaire   32
8. Madison   34
9. Caleb   36
10. Madison   39
11. Caleb   48
12. Madison   53
13. Caleb   60
14. Madison   70
   Saved by a Billionaire   73
15. Caleb   75
16. Caleb   80
17. Madison   82
18. Caleb   85
19. Madison   87
20. Caleb   89
21. Madison   91
22. Caleb   94
23. Madison   95
24. Caleb   98
25. Caleb   101
26. Madison   105
27. Caleb   107
   Sneak Peek - Chapter 1   109
   Chapter Two   115
   Chapter Three   120

©Copyright 2022 by Michelle Love - All rights Reserved

ISBN: 978-1-958151-35-8

In no way is it legal to reproduce, duplicate, or transmit any part of this document in either electronic means or in printed format.

Recording of this publication is strictly prohibited, and any storage of this document is not allowed unless with written permission from the publisher.

All rights are reserved.

Respective authors own all copyrights not held by the publisher.

❀ Created with Vellum

BLURB

He's rich as sin, naughty between the sheets.
And way too handsome for my own good.

I tried not to fall for him, but he was too hard to resist.

Every time he stares at me, he makes the air thin and hard to breathe.

His eyes are a shade of blue that looks as if it will freeze you and melt you all simultaneously.

My pulse quickens, and I feel the color springing into my cheeks.

It's so hard to take my eyes off his beautiful face.

He's got me mesmerized.

But I wonder if he'd be willing to save me from the man that keeps destroying everything I work for.

TAKEN BY A BILLIONAIRE
AN ALPHA BILLIONAIRE ROMANCE

Madison

There is a sea of men, in dark, tailored suits.

A sea of men that I now have to walk through.

We, my dear friend Kim and I, arrive at the new art gallery promptly at 1 o'clock. She is simply punctual like that.

With our high heels clicking and our perfume wafting, she and I walk up the steps in front of the building.

The men are all ages, all handsome, and all very rich. They nod in appreciation as we walk by, smiling, winking, nodding their heads.

Kim smiles a wide, minxish smile.

She's relishing it. Loving it.

And she's used to it, the admiring gazes. She's come to expect them always.

And why wouldn't they look? She's tall, leggy, blonde, and you can just feel the sex radiating off of her. Today she's wearing a sequined, body hugging dress. One that shows off all her curves.

She is a goddess.

I look down at my dress and tug at the hem one more time.

I too had dressed up. For fun. To make myself feel good.

But unlike Kim, I am not here for the attention. I'm here because she asked me to come to this event, the opening of a new gallery owned by one of her clients.

I wasn't in the market for a new painting or anything like that. But I thought the event had the potential to be an excellent networking opportunity. The art world and the music world were closely intertwined, after all.

Or so I thought.

One look around and I can tell this isn't my usual scene.

In any case, I decide to make the most of it.

Plus Kim is visiting from Chicago. She'd moved out there several years ago for work. She would be going home in a few days, and I wanted to spend as much time with her as possible.

We go inside and immediately grab two glasses of champagne.

My stomach growls. I'd only had coffee on the way out the door. I had practically run so that I could meet Kim here on time.

I turn to her. "Pastis for lunch?"

She doesn't hear me. She's too busy making sexy eyes at some tall, distinguished looking gentleman with salt-and-pepper hair. She raises her glass as he inclines his head toward her.

I roll my eyes. Then I grab her arm and start walking away, dragging her with me.

I know where this will lead. She'll find someone she wants to make a night of it with, and I'll be stuck talking to his dull friend.

Not today.

Kim may very well be on the prowl, but I am decidedly not.

Men always seem to bring trouble into my life. So I just try to keep my head down and focus on my work.

We waltz through the various rooms, eyeing paintings and sculptures.

Well, I'm eyeing the paintings and the sculptures.

Kim is eyeing the men. And there are plenty to choose from.

"What's going on over there?" Kim turns to me and asks.

There's a crowd forming in the room next to us. We walk over to see what the commotion is all about.

One piece, in particular, seems to be drawing a lot of attention. People are starting to bid on it and fight over it. An impromptu art auction springs up right there in the middle of the room.

Kim and I stand back to take in the action. She's whispering to me, saying something or other. But I'm sucked into the painting.

It's stunning. A tempestuous swirl of bold reds and calming yellows. Splashes of orange. It was as if the sun had burst and splattered itself onto the canvas.

The piece is causing quite a stir. And rightfully, so. If I had the money; I'd be making a play for it myself.

"Don't look now," Kim whispers to me, leaning in closer. "But there is a very cute stranger off to your left."

I start to roll my eyes. But then she adds, "And he seems to be quite taken with you."

This piques my interest. I glance to my left and immediately see who she's talking about.

I don't know how I missed him, even if I wasn't exactly looking.

He's the very epitome of tall, dark, and handsome.

And sure enough, he is looking right at me.

His silent stare makes the air thin and hard to breathe. My pulse quickens, and I can feel the color spring into my cheeks.

His hair is curly, dark, and hits just at the nape of his neck. His eyes are the shade of blue that looks as if it will freeze you and melt you all at the same time. His jawline is strong, absolute perfection.

It's so hard to take my eyes off his beautiful face, but I quickly turn away. I feel a little out of breath like I had just gotten off some thrill ride at an amusement park. I try, with great effort, to direct my attention back to the painting.

Kim raises an eyebrow at me. "You're not going to go over there?"

I shake my head, unable to speak for the moment.

I start to tell myself that I'm imagining the whole thing. That he's looking at someone behind me instead. There are plenty of other women there, after all. And it seems as though he has more than one new fan because I'm not the only one staring.

I take another glance in his direction. This time, the corners of his mouth turn up slightly, just barely showing the hint of a dimple.

He is definitely looking at me. And ignoring his fan club for the moment.

My belly does a flip-flop.

The next thing I know, Kim starts to drag me off in the opposite direction. "There's Maxim," she says.

Maxim is her client and owner of the gallery. He smiles when he sees her and waves us over.

"Come on," she says. "I'll introduce you to him."

As we walk off, I decide to steal one more glance over my shoulder. I can't help it.

I search the room looking for my handsome stranger.

But he's gone.

1

CALEB

I'd lost her.

I whip my head around frantically, trying to spot her in the crowd, but she's nowhere around.

A group of chatty older men had walked between us, obstructing my view.

And then she'd just disappeared.

I frown.

"What are you looking for?"

I turn toward Rob, one of my oldest friends and now business partner. "Did you see that woman?" I ask.

He laughs. "There are lots of women here." He follows a curvy redhead with his eyes as if to illustrate his point.

I shake my head. "Never mind."

I can't let it go, though.

She was exquisite. The most breathtaking woman I've ever seen.

My cock stirred the second I first laid eyes on her. I hoped no one had noticed.

I walk on into the next room with Rob. I keep an eye out and chide myself for not saying anything to my mystery woman earlier.

I try to concentrate on what I'm here to do, but it's proving difficult.

I was there at the art gallery with my partners. We had just moved our firm into new offices and thought some new artwork would be a good way to snazz up the place.

Plus we figured this was a good way to work on getting some new accounts.

Not that we needed any new accounts.

We were doing extremely well.

The rest of the financial world had taken to calling us the Rat Pack. "Rat" was an acronym for "retired at thirty."

And the way we were going, we could likely retire before that.

Brad, my other partner, and good friend walks up to me. "You want to see that show tomorrow? The one everyone's raving about?"

"I can't. I've got dinner with Bruce."

Bruce was our mentor. And we each had a standing one-on-one dinner date with him, as well as a group lunch, once every month.

We're standing off in the corner of the room talking to some man that Rob knows. I glance over and see out of the corner of my eye the tall blonde that my mystery woman was with earlier.

No sign of my mystery woman, though.

I nudge Brad. "Hey," I say, pointing to the tall blonde. "Do you know her?"

"No. But she's pretty hot. Why? Who is she?"

I sigh. "Never mind."

I could just go up and introduce myself, and then politely ask about her friend. But that would just get people talking. As it were, I already had a few women tailing me through the gallery, magically appearing wherever I was standing.

At the far end of the gallery, Brad begins making our final selections and arranging payment and delivery. We were all happy with the pieces he'd chosen so we let him handle the details.

I glance down at my watch. It's 3 o'clock, and this thing is winding down.

"The car is waiting out front," Brad says to me when he finishes with the gallery owner. "I'm just going to say bye. I'll meet you guys outside."

I am beyond ready to go, and so I make my way out front first. I stand at the top of the steps and take the time to light a cigarette while waiting for the rest of my group.

I had quit last month for the fifth time. But it wasn't taking.

That's when I see her.

My mystery woman.

She's getting into the back of sleek, black Lincoln, her tall friend right behind her. I have the overwhelming urge to call out to her, but I realize I don't know her name.

Still, my eyes are transfixed on her.

The car door slams and the wheels start to move.

In the exact moment the Lincoln rolls by, my mystery woman looks up.

It's just a quick glance, but our eyes meet through the car window.

And then she's gone.

Again.

I'd lost her for the second time.

2

CALEB

I arrive at the restaurant at seven o'clock on the dot.

I sit down at the table and order a glass of single malt while I wait for Bruce.

Twenty minutes and another scotch later I glance at my watch. I make an annoyed sound and tap my fingers on the table. I'm just about to go ahead and order without him.

A minute or so after I order my appetizer, Bruce comes walking up to the table and sits.

"You're late," I say, not even making an effort to hide my annoyance.

He gives a dismissive wave of his hand. "Only twenty minutes," he replies. "No big deal. Relax. So how was the opening?"

I smile, remembering my mystery woman and then fix my face when he gives me a curious look. "The usual," I reply. "Pretty boring actually. Got some nice pieces, though. Should liven the place up a little."

"Sounds good. Okay. What've you got for me?"

I reach into my briefcase and pull out my leather bound notebook and a stack of spreadsheets. We spend the next thirty minutes going over my specific goals for the quarter. After these strategy sessions, Bruce would check in with me weekly. Usually on Saturday afternoons. I'd update him on the progress of specific action items.

Bruce can be an asshole at times, but he knows what he's doing. And he knows how to keep me on track with whatever it is I am trying to achieve. He takes the time to teach. The guys and I are lucky to have him.

With the projections done, we relax and take the time to enjoy our meal. I put my notebook away into my briefcase as our entrees arrive at the table.

The server sets a sirloin steak, medium rare, with a side of steamed vegetables in front of me. Immediately, I begin to salivate.

"Be right back. I'm going to take a piss," Bruce says as he gets up from the table.

I shrug and take another bite of my steak. I'm happily engrossed in my meal when something else grabs my attention.

It's the scent that makes me look up from my plate.

Perfume..sweet, spicy, and faintly herbal. It isn't the scent itself but the fact that the scent is familiar to me. I try to rack my brain to remember where I know it from.

And then like magic, she enters into my view.

She walks into the restaurant with the same cougar friend she was with the previous day at the art gallery. The hostess walks them past my table and sits them down in the opposite corner near the kitchen.

It takes a little while before I can catch her eye.

She turns, she must have felt my eyes on her, and she glances at me briefly. I can see the recognition register in her face. Then, in a flash, she turns back to her friend.

I feel that familiar movement in my slacks again, and I shift uncomfortably in my seat.

I want to go over there, but Bruce would soon be on his way back from the restroom. I can never be sure how he'll act in situations like this. In general, I make it a point to keep anyone I'm interested in far away from him. If he knows I have my eye on this particular woman, he'll be likely to approach her and say something that will embarrass me, no doubt.

Or worse, he'll make a play for her himself.

I can't have that.

So I force my attention back to my steak and try to pretend she isn't there. I still take a glance here and there, but I try not to be obvious about it.

Now I have a dilemma.

I don't want my mystery woman to slip away again, but I don't want to put her on Bruce's radar either.

The server comes over to remove our plates, interrupting my train of thought. Bruce asks him for the check. "Right away, sir," he says.

I have to think fast. "I'd like to place a separate order to go if that's okay," I say to the server just before he turns away.

"Sure. What would you like, sir?"

"A steak salad please."

Ben raises his eyebrow at me.

"For my lunch tomorrow," I explain. "Don't feel like cooking."

He shrugs. "Expensive lunch."

The server returns a little while later with my salad packaged neatly in a brown paper bag. I hand him my black card. Ben seems distracted by something on his phone, so I seize my opportunity. I lean toward the server and speak to him in a low voice. "Please add whatever the ladies at the far table order to my tab." I motion toward their table, and then I slip a business card from my wallet and hand it to him. "And please give this to the young woman in the black dress."

The server smiles and gives me a slight nod. "I'll take care of it, sir."

Ben looks up from his phone. "You ready?"

I nod. We get up and start walking toward the front door.

I take one last, longing look at my mystery woman.

She's engrossed in conversation with her friend. I try to will her to look up, but she doesn't.

The door to the restaurant closes behind me.

All that's left for me to do is to hope that she'll actually call.

3

MADISON

I don't even notice him when I walk in.

But I feel his eyes on me.

Hot and prickly, like Superman with his heat vision.

Kim excuses herself just after our appetizers arrive. I start to dig into my salad, not wanting to wait for her to get back. It's a heavenly mix of fresh, ripe peaches, vine beans, cucumber, red onion, goat milk feta, and a harissa vinaigrette. Cool, crisp, and delicious.

Then all of a sudden...heat.

A warming sensation, traveling up my arm, up my neck and into my face.

I look over my shoulder, feeling suddenly very exposed.

And there he is.

The handsome stranger.

Our eyes meet. And just like that the rest of the room fades away.

He stops chewing. Then he puts his knife and fork down next to his plate and leans all the way back in his chair.

And then he just lets his baby blue eyes wash over me.

For the longest minute, I just stare at his face. My gaze travels from his piercing eyes down to his lips. In that very moment, he bites it, pulling his bottom lip between his teeth.

A slow smile spreads across his face, and his dimples are back in full force.

Lickable dimples.

My breath catches.

It's a look that says only one thing.

We both know I can make you faint with pleasure...

Kim returns to the table, and I quickly shift my attention back to my salad. For whatever reason, I don't want her to know that my handsome stranger is here in the restaurant with us. She'll probably just end up embarrassing me.

Or trying to take him for herself.

The whole time we eat, I force myself to keep my eyes on her.

But my mind keeps wandering to him.

"I'll get it," Kim says when the server arrives with the check. She starts to pull out her credit card.

"No need, ma'am," says the server, placing a gentle hand on her arm. "The bill has already been paid."

"By whom?"

"The gentleman at the far table."

We both turn to look in the direction the server is pointing, but there's no one there.

"That's funny," he says. "He was there a minute or two ago."

The server then leans in toward me and whispers, "He asked me to give you this, madame." He proceeds to place a card in my hand.

I blush and look down at it. It's an excellent quality. Clean design, heavy card stock and embossed lettering.

Caleb L. Jones, Financial Services, it reads.

I try to keep a neutral facial expression. I put the card down when Kim gives me a questioning look.

I shrug. "Guess we'll never know," I say.

"Free meal? We'll chalk that one up to a win."

It's almost ten when I make it back to my apartment. It had been a long day, and all I want now is a nice, hot shower before bed.

I pause, looking at my phone on the kitchen counter.

It isn't too late yet. Maybe my handsome stranger is still awake.

Over the next five minutes, I wrestle with the decision to call him or not. Finally, I grab my purse and begin looking for his card.

It isn't at the top of my bag where it should have been and after a good minute of rummaging, I still haven't found it.

I turn my purse over and frantically dump the contents of my bag out onto my bed.

No card.

I realize then that I'd left my handsome stranger's card at the restaurant.

I think briefly about calling the restaurant and after a minute of deliberation, I do just that.

Nothing.

They must have thrown it away when the table was being cleared, the person on the other line had said.

I hang up and sink into my bed, suddenly very moody.

I stay up for another hour wondering how I let my handsome stranger slip right through my fingers yet again.

4

CALEB

I slam the phone down hard.

Probably much harder than I need to.

This particular client, the one I'm on the phone with, is the ultimate pain in my ass.

I don't want to lose the account, though, so I have no choice but to make nice.

The others had since long left the building. I was in the office by myself.

I look down at my watch and sigh. It was past time to pack it in.

I'm still agitated, though, and I need to blow off some steam.

Rather than reach for a cigarette or the bottle of scotch I keep in my bottom desk drawer, I change into my sweats.

The gym is a short walk from my new office. I walk through the front door and give a nod to the gym owner, who is in the corner sweeping.

He nods right back and smiles at me. "The usual?"

I nod and smile. "The usual," I reply.

I'm a regular at this place. And my late night sessions with the punching bag are starting to become the thing of legends. Sometimes the owner, Gus, would leave me there and let me lock up.

I wrap up my wrists tightly and then I punch the bag for a good hour. I don't bother to hit the showers before I leave because my penthouse is close by.

The cool night air hits my skin as I exit the gym. I pull the hood of my sweatshirt up over my head. I'm feeling so much better, but then my phone starts to buzz with another text message. It's from the pain-in-the-ass client, and he's threatening to ruin my newfound good mood.

I'm not paying attention to where I'm going; I'm so lost in the phone. I don't see until it's too late, and I run smack into someone on the street.

Papers and things go flying all over the sidewalk. Quickly, I bend down to help pick them up.

It isn't until our hands touch that I realize what's happening.

I look up and all of a sudden it seems as though the entire world starts moving in slow motion.

My mystery woman..and just when I was beginning to think I'd never see her again.

She smiles. "Well, if it isn't my guardian angel."

Her voice is low and husky and music to my ears.

I chuckle at this and shake my head. "No...no guardian. Certainly no angel."

She smiles and nods, stuffing the last of her things into her purse. I reach out my hand to help her stand up. "We've got to stop running into each other like this," I say. When she doesn't answer, I add, "I was hoping I'd hear from you."

"Yeah," she starts. "I misplaced your business card. I think I left it at the restaurant."

I raise my eyebrow at her. Her excuse is beyond typical, and I expected a little more from her. Can't she come up with something better? But then I decide to give her the benefit of the doubt and see if maybe I do have a shot after all. "Where are you heading now?"

"I was actually just getting ready to hail a cab."

"Let me get one for you," I say and stick my hand out to flag one down for her.

I look down at my sweats and grimace. I was hardly presentable, hardly in any condition to even be thinking about taking this woman out.

But this is my mystery woman. And I'm not about to let her get away again. I put my hand down and turn to her. "Have you had dinner yet?"

She nods and looks away. "Yes."

"Dessert?"

She looks at me and shakes her head. "Skipping dessert tonight."

I can't tell if she's being coy or if she's just not that into me. "Okay, how about a drink then? There's a place right up the block. It's only a short walk from here."

She hesitates before answering, looking around and seeming at a loss for words.

My heart sinks. I'm convinced she's going to say no.

But then she agrees.

"Okay," she says finally.

I can't help the silly smile that comes and splits my face in two. I clap my hands together. "Great."

I grab her things, and we take the short walk up the block to the little bar.

"What's your name?" I ask her on the way there.

"Madison." She smiles and holds her hand out toward me, and I shake it.

"Madison," I say, her name rolling off my lips like sweet honey. "I'm Cal."

We get to the bar a few minutes later. The place is packed, much to my chagrin. I search the floor and then find two empty seats in the corner. I guide Madison over to that corner and sit her down. "What would you like?"

"What are you having?"

"What I always have. Scotch. Single malt. Neat."

"Then I'll have a scotch. Single malt. Neat."

I smile. I'm already starting to like this girl.

"I'll be right back," I say. "Don't go anywhere."

I go over to the bar and order the two scotches. "The best you have," I instruct the bartender.

He comes back with two glasses and shows me a bottle of the Macallan 18 year.

I nod. That would do.

I bring the two drinks back to the table and set hers in front of her.

She doesn't drink it right away. She sits and stirs it with her finger, eyes on me the whole time.

I take a sip of mine and try not to wrinkle my brow at her.

Did she not drink? Why wouldn't you say so?

"So what do you do?" I ask, attempting to start a conversation.

"I work in the recording industry."

"Doing what?"

"I have a record label."

She still hasn't touched her drink. She seems to be staring at something fascinating on her left hand.

"Is that what you've always wanted to do?"

She smiles, and then, to my relief, finally picks up her glass and takes a sip. "No. I wanted to be a nurse. I started nursing school and everything."

"So what happened with that?"

"Things change, you know?"

I nod at this, not able to take my eyes off her.

"My turn," she says. "Where are you from?"

"Is it that obvious that I'm not from around here?"

"Painfully."

"I'm from the Midwest originally, Illinois. Went to school out there But my parent moved out here to Jersey awhile ago. And you? You're a native New Yorker I'm guessing."

She takes another sip. "You guess correctly."

"What did you study in school?"

"Study?" I laugh. "Honestly most of it was a blur. I don't remember much studying going on. I do remember being proud of having learned how to sew."

Finally, I get a laugh out of her, and the mood instantly lightens. I reach out to touch her fingers and feel a jolt of electricity when her skin touches mine.

Some guy that had been watching us from the far corner comes over at that moment. He says hello to Madison, completely ignoring the fact that I'm sitting there.

He's drunk. Messy drunk. Slurring his speech drunk.

She tries to wave him away, but he stays put.

I can feel the trouble about to start. I would get Madison out of here and continue this another time, but he's blocking the direction of the entrance.

The only way to go is through him.

I take a deep breath and ready myself. Then I place my hand firmly on his arm. "Leave her alone," I say expecting him to just walk away.

But he doesn't do that.

Instead, he reaches out to punch me right in the face.

5

MADISON

It all happens so quickly.

All of a sudden everyone is fighting and throwing themselves all over the place.

I try to keep out of the way and attempt to scream to Cal that we need to go, but he doesn't hear me.

At least he's winning the fight.

That is until the big ugly drunk guy breaks a bottle, brandishing the jagged edge as a weapon.

Shit just got real.

. . .

Cal backs off a little, but only just a little. He glances around, and I can tell he's looking for a weapon for himself to even up the playing field.

Big Ugly snarls and then smiles. He thinks he has Cal beaten, and so he turns his attention back toward me. He comes over and grabs my arm and that's when I deck him square on the jaw.

But he doesn't let go so I grab a heavy napkin dispenser with my free hand, and I hit him over the head with it.

Big Ugly slumps to the ground. Cal looks at me, clearly shocked. I step forward and tug on his arm. "Come on! We need to go." I don't want to be there when Big Ugly wakes up, which could be any minute now.

I drag Cal out through the front door, our bodies stumbling into one another's.

His hand is on his back, and when it comes away, it's covered in red.

"You're bleeding," I say. "We should get you to the hospital."

"No," he shakes his head. "I'll be okay. My apartment is right around the corner. I'll be okay as soon as I get home."

. . .

I look at him uncertainly. "Your apartment is around the corner?"

He nods.

"You took me to a bar that was right around the corner from your place? Were you trying to get lucky?"

He smiles and then winces in pain. I know I'm in trouble because one glance at that smirk makes me dizzy. And if I was annoyed a second ago, I'm not anymore.

"No," he says. "Just hoping."

"Okay," I say. "Let me help you."

I put his arm around my neck, and we both stumble along the two blocks to his apartment. I think for a second about whether I really should help him upstairs, but in the end I decide to be a good Samaritan.

We get into the elevator, and he puts in a key, next to the big "P" for penthouse and turns it.

Up we go to the top floor. I chew on my lip, wondering if I'm making a mistake by coming up here with him. I tell myself that he's wounded and that if he did try anything, I could easily best him.

.   .   .

The elevator opens right into the middle of a sprawling living room. I let out a low whistle. "Nice place."

It's easily three, maybe four times bigger than my own place. Littered with expensive looking things; leather, wood, crystal. The rugs look like they come from overseas. In fact, the whole place looks like something you'd see in a travel magazine.

"You live here by yourself?"

He doesn't hear me because he's rummaging through his things looking for some bandages. He stumbles back over to where I am sitting by the living room coffee table. "Let me see it," I say

He nods and then pulls his now bloodied t-shirt over his head. I try not to look at his pecs or his abs. Just the wound on his back.

"You're not saying anything back there. How does it look?"

Big Ugly had gotten him real good. "You're going to need stitches."

He lets out a hiss.

.   .   .

"Well," I start. "You were bragging about knowing how to sew earlier. So where's your stuff?"

He jerks his head to the side. "Top drawer on the right."

I go over to the drawer, look through it and then pull out a small sewing kit. "Any vodka?"

"You're drinking at a time like this?"

"For you, silly."

He motions to the back of the room. "Bar's over there."

I pull out a bottle of vodka and first pour a little on my hands to sanitize them. Then I give him the bottle. "Here. You might want to take a swig."

He grabs the bottle from me and takes a long swallow.

I take it back from him. "This is going to hurt," I say as I dab some of the alcohol onto his cut. He winces but he doesn't cry out.

I proceed to sew him up taking care to keep the stitches small.

"You sure you know what you're doing back there?"

. . .

I scoff at this. "You're the one that didn't want to go to the hospital."

"Yeah, well if you leave a scar, I'm suing you. I don't care that you're not a professional."

"You really want to make jokes with me? I'm the one holding the needle here."

"Right. I should stay on your good side. That's a mean right cross you've got."

I finish up, snip the thread and lean back to admire my work.

"What's the prognosis, Doc?"

"You'll live," I say.

He nods. "Good."

I stand and walk around to face him. His face is a little pale, but he's still gorgeous as hell. He looks up at me and smiles. My skin tingles where his eyes linger. His smile doesn't lessen the intensity of his gaze. If anything, the smile holds an even darker promise.

. . .

I need to leave.

"Well, Jones," I start. "You certainly do know how to show a lady a good time."

He chuckles at this.

"I'm not being funny," I add. "I genuinely haven't had that much fun on a first date in forever. It's been ages since I've been in a good fight."

His smile widens and my knees threaten to buckle.

"Plus, I did get to see you with your shirt off, so the night wasn't a total bust."

"I know I've probably blown it," he says. "But I really want to see you again." It's a lusty whisper.

"You will," I say and then turn toward the door. "I should get home. You get some rest. Have a good night, Cal."

He gets up to walk me over to the door.

But we don't quite get there because he falls over and passes out.

6

MADISON

I really want to go home but, I can't leave him here like this.

I shake my head and guide him back to the couch. And then I sit and try to relax and make myself at home.

While I'm here, I may as well pour myself another drink.

I tell myself that I'll just watch him for a little while to make sure he doesn't die and then I'm going to let myself out.

A minute later, he wakes. His hair all ruffled. I can tell it takes him a minute to register everything that's happened.

"How are you feeling?"

. . .

He rubs his head. "I'm okay," he says. I'm not sure if he is trying to convince me or if he's trying to convince himself.

"Good," I say. "And now that you're feeling better, I'm gonna go ahead and leave. You should eat something, by the way."

I get up to go, and he gets up too.

It's his hand on my arm that stops me. The way he grips my wrist.

Firm.

Commanding.

I turn and face him. The heat in his gaze is unmistakable.

"No," he says. "Stay."

My eyes are locked on his and I cannot look away. The warmth from his hand travels slowly up my arm like a flame would creep up the fuse on a stick of dynamite.

And like that dynamite, I was about to blow.

. . .

Cal takes a step closer, reaches out with his other hand, and rests his thumb on my lower lip.

Then he leans in.

I should step back.

I don't know him.

He could be an ax murderer for all I know.

But I'm frozen in place, my feet glued to the floor.

Too late to run.

His lips fall onto mine. And I kiss back.

His breath is warm on my cheek, and it lights the little hairs on my body on fire. His kiss is insistent, but his lips are soft. He grabs my other arm and pulls me even closer to him.

He pulls back slightly and softly flicks his tongue against my lips, teasing a small moan from my mouth.

. . .

Then he stops and looks at me, the corners of his mouth turning up into a knowing smile.

I'd showed him my hand. He knows he has me now.

There's something in those blue eyes that excites me and makes me feel..I don't know what, but I want to find out.

"I've been wanting to do that for quite some time," he says.

Suddenly, though I don't know how, I find my feet. I try to walk away but the next thing I know, his arms are tightly around me, my feet are off the floor, and I'm being carried into his bedroom.

My head is racing, and I can't believe how quickly I've lost control of this situation. What is happening? I need to slow this down.

"Wait–"

I hardly get the word out because then his lips crash into mine once more.

My feet touch the floor again, but he doesn't let go. He pulls back and looks me in the eye, his intentions crystal clear.

. . .

He must sense my hesitation. "Do you want to go?" he asks.

The way he holds me firmly in place with his gaze...the way he smiles. I know I'm not going anywhere.

We both do.

Besides it's been awhile. My body needs this.

7

CALEB

I wasn't trying to get laid on the first date.

Honest.

But something just came completely over me.

Maybe I'm just lightheaded due to the loss of blood.

The truth is I can't think straight around her. Being in her space... the way she looks..the way she moves...her low, throaty voice...the smell of her.

Drives me fucking crazy.

I had every intention of being the perfect gentleman, of being polite, waiting, and making sure she was comfortable.

But all that went out the window the minute she set foot in my penthouse.

Stitches or no stitches, I have to have her.

Tonight.

Right now.

In a second my hands are all over her, exploring all her soft curves.

I search her eyes for consent and can see she's still not sure.

But then the way she looks at me in the next second...like she'd let me do whatever I wanted to her...that does it.

I lift her hands above her head to remove her shirt in one sweeping motion.

Her breasts, full and perky and clad in a sexy black lace bra graze against my bare chest. Immediately, I put my arms up, cupping one in each hand. Squeezing. Kneading.

She throws her head back with a moan and then slips one of her hands down the front of my sweatpants. She gives a slight gasp when she feels my girth and almost pulls her hand away. But I hold her still. She's not going to get away again. Not tonight.

I suck her bottom lip between mine and she relaxes against me again. Then we topple over onto my bed. I press my full weight on her, and she spreads her legs and starts to grind slowly against me.

She has on too much clothing, I decide. I pull back and unbutton her jeans. They may as well have been painted on, they were so snug. Then I drop them to the floor.

I lick my lips and kiss up her thighs and her stomach, inch by inch, very slowly.

She laces her fingers into my hair and tugs gently. When I look up at her, she bites her bottom lip.

I can tell she's enjoying this. I can tell she wants it. But she won't get it. Not just yet. I want this in no uncertain terms. I want her to know what is about to go down. I want her to want it as badly as I do.

I make one more round of kisses around her lower belly and hip area. And then slowly I slide her panties off and kiss back up her inner thighs.

She lifts her hips slightly and inches them closer and closer to me, but I hold my hand out to steady her. "Stay still," I say.

She lets out an exasperated moan and lowers her hips back onto the bed. I take the time to kiss all around her inner thighs, the top of her mound, her lower stomach.

Everywhere but.

She's grabbing at the sheets, tugging them, and I can tell she's about to lose it.

Slowly and very gently, I offer her the very tip of my tongue. Her back arches immediately, and she lets out a loud moan.

"You like that? You want more of it?"

She doesn't answer.

I stop. "I asked you a question."

"Yes," she says, barely getting the word out.

Then I bury my head between her legs.

She was delicious, like a cross between an avocado and a mango.

Creamy.

Sweet.

She fights back a moan and pushes her hips against my face. Her thighs start to vibrate on each one of my cheeks.

I know she's close. So, I speed up, flicking as fast as my tongue would go. She's full on screaming now. Her whole body tenses up, and I know she's about to come. The stream hits me in the next instant, flowing over my tongue and I lap it all up like a thirsty dog.

I give her a minute to let her catch a breath, to let her body still the quivering.

Then she looks up at me with unadulterated 'fuck me' eyes.

And I know I can't wait any longer.

I grab her thighs and bend her legs back almost to her ears. Then I slide into her with one motion.

"Christ..." I mutter. "You feel so...fucking...good." I punctuate each syllable with a deep thrust.

Her perfectly manicured nails sink into the flesh on my shoulders as she stretches to accommodate me.

I'm up on my elbows now, pumping faster. As my thrusts get harder, her moans get louder. Her back is arching, her skin takes on a beautiful flush, and I know she's going to come again.

"I can feel you coming," I whisper.

Then her orgasm hits me in a wave. Her hands wrap around my

waist, pushing me deeper into her as she grinds her hips up and against mine.

I'm right behind her. I can feel myself about to explode. I try to pull out, but she doesn't let me. She grabs my ass tighter and presses me into her. "No," she pants. "Come inside me."

My eyes go wide. It's the last thing in the world I expected her to say. But I don't have time to think about it because all my muscles start to clench, and I let loose right there inside her.

I'm panting. She's panting.

I collapse on top of her and then roll off, my arm still around her waist, while we both catch our breath.

After a few minutes, she starts to move but I reach out to her, tighten my grip on her. She nods, understanding that I want her to stay the night with me.

In the next minute, she closes her eyes and falls asleep.

Again, I'm right behind her.

The next morning when I wake, she's gone.

To be continued...

DESIRED BY A BILLIONAIRE
AN ALPHA BILLIONAIRE ROMANCE

Caleb

I must not hear when the alarm goes off, because when I wake, it's already almost ten o'clock.

Oh well. Work can wait.

I stretch out in bed, not yet opening my eyes to the blinding sun.

Instinctively, I reach over.

Nothing.

The sheets are empty, cold, and barely even wrinkled.

I immediately sit up straight. My head is pounding. My heart is beating quickly, and confusion is starting to set in.

I get up slowly out of my bed and head over to the bathroom. She's not there. Nor is she in the living room or the kitchen.

There's no note, no message on my phone.

She's gone. Vanished into thin air.

I start to try and call but then I realize that she never gave me her number.

I'm a bonafide hit and run.

Damn it.

I don't know how to feel about this. I close my eyes and images from the previous night pop into my head. Her in her black lace bra and panties. Her on her back in my bed. Her on top of me. Her pulling me closer and breathlessly calling my name.

It had to be real. Had to be.

Why fake it with me?

My phone rings and I nearly trip over myself to answer it.

It's not her; it's the office.

"Everyone's looking for you," I hear Robert's worried voice come over the line. "Where the hell are you man? Is everything OK?"

"I had a late night," I say, suddenly very weary despite sleeping in late. "Just cover for me. I'll be there in a little while."

I drag myself into the shower and then force myself to get ready. It was going to be hard to face the day; I could feel it.

It would be better if I knew where to find her. But I don't. I don't know where she lives, or works. I don't know anyone who knows her. Hell, I don't even know if Madison is her real name come to think of it.

She may as well be a ghost.

I'd lost her again, let her slip right through my fingers. Maybe it's just not meant to be.

I turn the shower off, grab my robe, and go back to the kitchen. I make myself a nice, strong cup of black coffee.

By the time I shave, dress, and get the dimples in my tie just perfect, I'm feeling much better.

This woman apparently does not know who I am.

I am Caleb Jones, and I get what I want.

And I want her.

So that's it. I'm going to find her, plain and simple.

And when I do, I'm going to teach her not to walk away from me.

8

MADISON

I feel a slight pang of guilt when I hang up the phone.

I never, ever call out of work. I've always been responsible, too responsible if that's even a thing. When I was younger people used to tell me, I was too serious for a girl my age.

My answer was always the same.

You had to be serious when you were forced to grow up as fast as I did.

I lay back down and tell myself that I'm the boss and that it's OK for me to take some time for myself if I need to.

And I do.

I need a moment to breathe. And to relax. And to process just what the hell happened last night, what went on between Cal and me.

I feel the heat rise in my cheeks the instant I start to think about him.

I didn't know it could be this way. So good. So bad.

So painful and yet so exhilaratingly pleasurable all at the same time.

My experiences with sex had been mediocre at best up to now.

Most men didn't seem to know what they were doing, didn't seem to even want to know what they were doing.

But Cal...

Cal was a masterful lover. Patient. Skilled. Gentle at times but commanding at others. He'd taken me on a thrill ride of emotion last night.

I stretch and then wince at the delightful soreness blooming between my legs.

I'm still embarrassed at my actions, but I had to admit that I also felt good.

That he felt good.

Call him, Madison. What harm could it really do?

I stop this line of thinking as soon as it starts.

It could do lots of harm, actually, I tell myself. I shouldn't even be thinking about this.

If I allow myself to get close to him, then just like that he can find out about all my 'stuff'.

And what then?

Would he still want me?

I grimace at the thought. It was doubtful that he would.

I'm safer where I am, which is far away from Caleb Jones. He doesn't know me and doesn't know where to find me. I don't think I even mentioned the name of my company.

I could just fade into the background and pretend that last night never even happened.

9

CALEB

I know it's her the second I see her. Her back is facing me, but I recognize her shape, her long, wavy blond mane.

It had been two weeks since I'd seen her last. I was beginning to give up hope. But now here she is.

I start to walk faster. She's headed in the opposite direction, which isn't totally a bad thing. Her dress, though professional, is form-fitting, hugging that perfect ass in all the right ways. She looks so good from behind, the way her hips sway when she walks.

I'd have slowed down if she wasn't walking so fast.

I should be angry, but I'm not. I quicken my pace so that I can catch her.

Even in her heels she's speed walking. When I get just a pace or two behind her, she turns and is about to cross the street and so I reach out and grab her arm.

She spins, anger flashing in her green eyes and for a second she looks like she's about to swing on me. "What the..." but then she trails off when she sees me and her jaw drops.

"Hey."

What are you doing here?" she asks.

I laugh at this. "Am I not allowed to walk on this street?"

She blushes. "That's not what I meant."

"You meant that you never expected to see me again. Is that right?"

She doesn't answer.

"My office is a block or so from here," I say. "I was just about to grab some lunch."

"Oh," she replies. She looks down at her shoes, and I take a step closer. She looks back up. "My office is in the area too."

Our offices are close together. Noted. Though she doesn't seem all that excited about it.

"Why did you take off? I was looking forward to waking up next to you."

"I had a really early appointment," she says quickly.

I know she's lying.

I'm not sure why, but I decide to let it slide for the moment.

"Have lunch with me."

She turns and looks back down the block; she looks uneasy. Unsure.

"Come on," I urge. "You can step out for a bit. I'm sure they won't miss you." I smile at her. I find her nervousness unbearably cute. That seems to do it.

"OK," she says.

I take her by her arm and we walk a short distance to a coffee shop in the area. We sit by the window, and both decide on a salad.

She picks at her food, and I frown.

"Don't worry," I say after a long and awkward silence. "I won't press charges."

She looks up, confusion written all over her face. "I'm sorry," she says. "I'm afraid I don't follow."

"I won't press charges," I repeat. "Against you."

"For?"

"For drugging me and date raping me that night."

She drops her fork and looks confused for a long moment. Then I break into a broad smile, and she bursts out laughing. She laughs so loud that the sound fills the tiny coffee shop. Several people shoot disapproving looks in our direction.

"That was a good one, Jones."

Instantly, she loosens up. So I decide to take my shot.

"Listen," I begin.

"Uh, oh."

"I know I blew it the other night. It wasn't at all my idea of what a first date should be."

"I told you," she says. "I had fun." She blushes a little, and I catch her meaning.

"Still," I continue. "Let me make it up to you."

She raises her eyebrow.

"I'd like to take you to a proper dinner."

She doesn't say anything at first, just studies my face.

"This is the part where you agree to have dinner with me," I help her along.

"When?"

"Tonight. I'll send a car for you around 8 o'clock."

"OK."

"OK?"

"Learn to take yes for an answer, Jones."

And with that she gets up and saunters toward the door. "I need to get back to work. Thanks for lunch." And then over her shoulder she calls, "I'll see you tonight.

Yes, tonight.

10

MADISON

I adjust my dress one more time in the mirror. It's tighter than I'm used to, but it's the nicest one I have.

I reach for my lipstick and apply another coat. And then another small spritz of perfume for good measure.

The butterflies in my stomach are on overdrive.

Why am I so nervous?

I shouldn't even be doing this in the first place. I recall the stern talk I had with myself the other day.

He was right. I hadn't expected to see him again.

.   .   .

And I hadn't expected my panties to moisten instantly when I did.

I already agreed. So it would be rude to back out now, I tell myself.

I grab my hand lotion from my purse. I notice that my palms are starting to sweat.

Why? Why should I be afraid of him?

The door buzzes at 8 'clock on the dot.

I take a deep breath and then head down the stairs.

A sleek, black Mercedes with tinted windows is parked out front. Beside it, a man is standing with his hands folded. I can only assume this is Cal's driver.

I walk up to him, and he smiles and gives a slight nod of his head as I approach. "Good evening madam," he says with a deep, mature voice.

"Hello."

He walks over to the passenger side door and opens it for me. Then he holds my hand as I step inside.

.   .   .

When did this become my life?

We drive for around thirty minutes before the car comes to a stop. "This is your destination, madam," says the driver. "Enjoy your dinner."

He gets out to let me out of the car and motions to the front door of the building.

I walk in and go up one flight of stairs. There's a large door on the landing, and I assume it's the one I need to go through.

I gasp, and immediately I start to think I'm in the wrong place because it's empty.

It's a restaurant alright, but no one is there.

It's then that I see Cal, standing in the far corner of the room, and staring out of a large, floor to ceiling window.

I watch him for a second, study him. I smile to myself and then walk over to him.

The view of the city from the window is breathtaking.

. . .

He turns to me when I reach his side and lets out a low whistle. "You look beautiful," he says with a smile. He leans in and kisses me lightly on the cheek. "I trust the ride was good."

"Yes, it was," I reply, still a little overwhelmed by this whole scene. "Um, where is everybody?"

He turns to me and flashes that smile again, and my knees threaten to buckle. "It's just us tonight," he says.

"Just us? What does that mean?"

He throws his head back and laughs. "It means I bought the place out. My good friend here was good enough to accommodate my request. It means no interlopers. No interruptions. Just you. And me. Some good wine and a good meal."

He puts his hand on the small of my back and guides me toward the middle of the room. "We can sit at any table you want," he says.

I choose the table closest to the window, and we sit.

I take in the ambiance. Low light, candles, fresh flowers. There's some music in the background, something instrumental.

"You like?" he asks.

.　.　.

"Yes," I smile. "This is a very nice place."

He hands me a menu. "Would you like to choose the wine?"

I wave my hands. "No, no. Please, go ahead. I defer to you on such things."

He smiles. I think he likes the idea of me deferring to him.

He orders a bottle and the waiter nods and shuffles off. He comes back a minute later with the wine. He pours a little in Cal's glass. Cal picks it up, swirls it, sniffs it, and then nods his head. Cal then fills my glass, keeping his eyes on me the entire time.

I shift in my chair.

"OK. So it is me," he says.

"Pardon?"

"You tense up around me," he continues. "I thought it might be other people, or large groups or maybe just where we were. But now we're alone, and you're still tense. So it must be me."

I don't know how to answer this.

.   .   .

"Is it because of..."

"No," I say quickly. "It's not that. And I'm not tense. I just don't think we have anything in common."

He's amused by this because the corners of his mouth turn up into that sexy smile of his. "Try me."

I take a sip of my wine. And then another.

"Well," I start. "You're probably from Harvard and all."

He laughs at this and takes a sip of his wine.

"Probably some frat boy too."

He nods. "Yes as a matter of fact, I did go to Harvard business school. And yes, I did pledge Beta Theta Pi in undergrad. So what? A man's still got to eat right?"

I blush. "Right."

.   .   .

At that moment, our food comes. "I ordered for us in advance," he says.

The meal looks wonderful. A large braised short rib over a generous helping of creamy polenta with greens on the side. "Italian," I say. "My favorite."

"See?" he says with a smile. "We do have something in common."

After dinner, he asks if I'm planning on skipping dessert tonight. I agree to split one with him, and he orders something chocolatey.

"I love chocolate."

"Another thing we have in common," he says. "Careful. You might start to think that a scrappy Brooklyn girl and an Ivy League frat boy may actually be compatible."

He's making fun of me, but I don't mind.

After dessert and our second bottle of wine, I'm feeling friendly.

A little too friendly.

I don't want to end up back at his apartment again.

.   .   .

I mean I do, but I don't.

He must sense my anxiety because he says, "I'm not holding you hostage here. You can go home whenever you wish. Just say the word and I'll have my driver bring the car around."

I nod. "Yes. Dinner was lovely. But it's getting late, and I'm ready to go."

He nods. "Will you at least let me ride with you?"

"It's his car so I don't think I can actually say no, but I agree.

When we get in the car, I give the driver the address to my office. Cal gives me a skeptical look. "You're going back to work?"

"I forgot something. I just need to stop in and get it. I can make my way home from there."

He doesn't say anything.

It's his look, the way his eyes seem to see right through me.

That's what scares me so much.

.   .   .

We pull up in front of my office a short while later. I get out of the car, and he gets out as well. We walk toward the front door.

"I had a nice time, Jones."

"I'm glad."

I turn to him. He's looking me dead in the eye. The heat in his gaze is threatening to melt me down to nothing right there on the sidewalk. Like a magnet, I lean in toward him but then I catch myself and take a step back before he can get his arm around me. "Goodnight," I whisper. Then I turn and walk away.

"When can I see you again?" he calls from behind me.

I pause in the doorway and smile at him. "Call me?"

He looks confused for a second.

"I put my number in your phone."

He immediately grabs at his pocket and thumbs through his cell. A wide smile appears on his face.

I smile back and then go through the door, letting it close behind me.

11

CALEB

"Mr. Jones...Mr. Jones?"

I give a start in my chair. "Yes."

Everyone around the conference table is looking at me expectantly.

"I'm sorry. Can you repeat that?"

"What do you think about the proposal on the Bergman account?"

I'd zoned out. I wasn't even sure what was on the table.

"Whatever the group thinks best," I say. "Excuse me." I get up from the table and walk out of the conference room.

I need air. I leave the building to step outside.

I'm not alone with my thoughts for long. Rob and Brad come running up to me. "Meeting over already?" I ask them.

"Well, there wasn't much to say after you'd made your grand exit," laughed Rob, clapping me on the back.

"C'mon lets go get lunch," Brad says and then walks off in the direction of our favorite spot.

"So what's up with you man," he asks me when we get settled in.

"What do you mean?"

"You've been on another planet lately," he continues. "You completely checked out in that meeting just now."

I shrug. I'm allowed my off days like everyone else.

"It's that girl," says Rob with a smile.

"Oooh," says Brad. He turns to me. "You mean the sexiest woman alive? Is that what you call her?"

They're teasing me. "Yes, her," I say.

"She let you fuck her yet?"

I nearly choke on my salad. It isn't the question itself that catches me off guard.

It's my reluctance to answer it.

Normally, I'd be more than eager to brag to my friends about my latest conquest. I'd spare no detail. Where we did it, what kind of underwear she had on, whether she gave good head, what positions we did it in... I didn't care. Everything and everyone was fair game.

But now I'm finding that I want to remain tight-lipped where Madison is concerned.

Which could only mean one thing.

She'd really gotten to me.

And I guess I knew all along, but it's only now that I'm silently admitting it to myself.

I look up from my salad plate. "A gentleman never tells,"I say with a smile.

The other two break out into a chorus of raucous laughter.

"Oh you must have it bad this time playboy," laughed Rob.

I don't answer and instead concentrate hard on my plate. While they're laughing, I start to wonder what exactly it is I need to do to get Madison to spend the night with me again.

I stir the pot one more time and then set the sauce to simmer. I pace one, twice, three times around my kitchen, and then finally I pick up the phone.

Even though I couldn't stop thinking about her, I hadn't called. I didn't want to scare her off. But I couldn't wait any longer.

She picks up on the third ring.

"Hello."

"Hey," I say.

"Cal?"

"You were expecting someone else?"

She giggles on the other line. "No. To what do I owe the pleasure?"

"I just wanted to say hello."

"Well hello."

"And to see if you were hungry."

"Right now?"

"Yes, right now. I'm making dinner, and I wanted to know if you'd come eat with me."

"You cook?"

"Sure do. Learned from my mother. Though my cooking will never be as good as hers is."

Silence on the other line.

"Hello?"

"I'm here."

"So...dinner?"

Again, she doesn't answer.

"I can send the car to pick you up."

"No," she says finally, and my heart sinks.

"No?"

"No, you don't have to send the car. I know the way. I'll be there in an hour."

I almost jump into the air but try to sound cool on the phone. "Ok. I'll see you then."

She arrives just after 8 o'clock. The elevator door opens, and she takes a few soft steps into the living room. "Cal?"

"Over here," I say, calling to her from the kitchen.

She smiles and walks over to me. She sets a black plastic bag on the island.

"Moonshine?"

"No, silly. Wine. Wasn't sure if you wanted a red or a white so I got one of each. I hope I picked the right ones."

"I'm sure whatever you bought is fine," I say motioning for her to come closer. "Here, taste this." I hold out the wooden spoon I was stirring my sauce with.

She comes closer and parts her lips a little before wrapping them around the spoon. She closes her eyes, and a satisfied look spreads across her face. "Mmm." She licks her lips. "Delicious."

I fight to control myself. Watching her lips...

But the stove is still on, and the last thing I need to do is to burn down my penthouse.

"Almost done," I say, turning away from her so that she can't see the erection threatening to grow in my pants. "Make yourself comfortable. Dinner will be ready in a minute."

She walks back to the living room, kicks her shoes off and plops down right in the middle of my plush, sheepskin rug.

I smile. When the sauce is finished, I make two plates of pasta and pour some on. Then I grab one of the bottles of wine, two glasses and bring it all to the living room on a tray.

"No don't get up," I say to her. "We can eat here."

I'm letting her eat on my rug...I do have it bad.

I set her plate in front of her and pour us some wine. She dives right in, smiling as she chews.

I let out a small laugh.

"What?" she demands.

I shake my head. "Just seems like it's been forever since I've seen a woman really eat that's all."

"Oh." She looks confused for a minute. "Is that good?"

"Very."

I scoot a little closer to her and top up her wine glass. She holds my gaze for a split second and shifts her eyes around the room. They settle on my coffee table.

"You play Scrabble?" she asks, her face lighting up. I turn and see that she's eyeing my deluxe Scrabble board.

"You want some of this, Brooklyn? Alright, let's play."

I let her win. At least that's what I tell myself. I put the board away and then move even closer to her on the rug. She leans back until she's leaning against the couch. There's nowhere for her to go so I lean all the way in and kiss her softly.

For a minute, we seem lost in each other.

But then she pulls away. I don't understand the look she gives me. She looks frightened. As if she thinks I'm going to hurt her.

"I should go," she says and all of a sudden the mood is very different.

I want to protest, but I have a feeling if I press, she'll still run away and then who knows when the next time I see her will be.

"Sure," I say after a minute. "I'll have my driver take you home."

12

MADISON

I spread all the way out in my office chair until my hands and feet are hanging off of it.

I don't recall ever being so horny in my life.

Is blue balls for women a thing? Because if it is I surely have it now.

For the umpteenth time, I ask myself why I ran out of there so quick. Why I didn't stay.

I got nothing.

I bang my head against the desk. It seems like this day isn't ever going to end.

·   ·   ·

I tell myself for the umpteenth time that I should just forget about Cal.

But something also tells me it might be a little late for that.

I can't believe I didn't fuck him…

I look again at the clock on my desk. It's time to go. So what if I'm taking off a little early?

I grab my purse and leave, locking up behind me. I need a drink.

My stomach grumbles.

And some food.

I stop in at the gourmet burger spot to place a to-go order. "A deluxe please," I tell the man at the counter. And then, though I'm not sure why, I add, "Make that two."

I grab two Belgian ales from the fridge and wait for my order.

When the food is done, I pay the bill and then head back out onto the street.

·   ·   ·

I'm walking but not in the direction of my place.

My office is near Cal's.

And Cal's office is near his penthouse.

So that means, logically, that I am near Cal's penthouse.

My feet take me in that direction before I can think too much about it. And before I know it, I'm in front of his high rise.

And then I'm going through the door.

And then I'm in the elevator on the way up.

I should call maybe. What if there's another girl there?
    I knock once, twice, three times on the door.

No answer.

Maybe he's at the gym?

I'm being silly, showing up here like this. I turn to leave.

. . .

I get maybe two steps away before I hear the door open behind me. "Madison?"

I turn on my heels and start to speak. But then I see him standing there topless and wrapped in nothing but a bath towel, and suddenly there are no words.

He smiles, and my cheeks start to burn. "What are you doing here?" he asks.

"Well," I start, struggling to find words that don't sound lame. "I was in the neighborhood and...well I thought I'd pick up a couple of burgers"

He doesn't answer at first, and the silence gets to me quickly. "I'm sorry,"I stammer. "I probably shouldn't be here, shouldn't have come by unannounced. I'm going to go." I turn to leave, but his voice calls me back.

"The hell you are," he says. Then his smile widens, and his dimples deepen. "I'm hungry." He steps aside and lets me into the apartment.

"I'll be right back," he says. "Let me go put some clothes on."

I almost pout, almost tell him not to, but I will my mouth to stay shut. He comes back a minute later donning a button down and some jeans. "So what did you bring me?" he asks.

· · ·

I lay the food out onto the kitchen counter, and he walks over and hugs me from behind.

I freeze for a second; the move is so unexpected, but then I ease into the embrace and let my body relax against his.

"The sauce is for the fries," I say when he grabs at the tiny plastic cup. "Here, let me show you." I take one of the fries, dip it in the sauce and hold it out for him. He grabs the fry between his teeth and makes a satisfied sound. Then he holds onto my hand and sucks my finger into his mouth.

My breath catches. He keeps his eyes locked onto mine as he pulls my finger slowly out of his mouth.

He leans in, and it looks as though he's going to kiss me and I hold my hand against his chest.

He stands back and looks at me.

He smiles slowly. "I know what it is."

"Know what?"
"You want me to work for it?"

· · ·

"Pardon?"

He backs up, takes his hands off me, and suddenly I feel a chill. "OK," he says.

"OK, what?"

"OK. I'll work for it."

I shake my head. "I'm not naive. You only want one thing."

His smile is back, and I don't know if that's a good thing or a bad thing. "No, not naive," he says. "Unimaginative maybe. I can think of a hell of a lot more than one thing I want, starting with those lips."

He leans in again and before I can protest, his lips are on mine. I don't try to break away this time; I just let myself enjoy it.

When he pulls away, he whispers into my ear, "Thank you for dinner. You can go ahead and go home now if that's what you want."

I open my mouth to protest, but he stops me.

"No. Go ahead."

.   .   .

Then he leans in so close his lips graze the corner of my mouth "But make no mistake, Madison. You are mine. And I will have you again. Mark my words."

13

CALEB

The night is hot and humid

Thankfully, though, the beer is ice cold.

I press the cool bottle to my forehead in an attempt to cool myself down.

I'm hot.

But it isn't just the thick New York air.

It's her.

She has me hot.

And while this isn't anything new, it's extra unbearable on this particular night.

I'm a man who prides myself on my impeccable self-control.

But this girl...

She is about to make me lose it. And I'm not sure how I feel about that.

One part of me wants the dam to burst.

The other part struggles to hold on, afraid of what it will mean if I let her win.

I press the bottle to my forehead again.

It isn't working.

There's only one thing that will work. And I know that now.

I'll have to let her win.

After a fashion, of course.

I don't hear the soft footsteps approaching me. But I do smell her, and a few seconds later, she appears in my peripheral.

It's like she's reading my mind.

I'd asked her to meet me for a beer in the little bar downstairs from me. She agreed.

She sidles up and sits on the empty bar stool next to me, with something of a smirk on her face. She puts a slim cigarette between her full lips. I smile, reach into my pocket for my lighter, and then light it for her.

"Two more," I say to the bartender when he walks by. He nods, and I turn my attention back to the puzzle in front of me.

"Hot tonight," she says, her voice low and throaty, a slow smile spreading across her face.

I nod, grinning. "Indeed."

Had she been just about any other woman, I'd have taken her by now.

Countless times.

But she's different.

Special. Though I say that somewhat grudgingly.

And while I can't deny that my body responds to her in the most intense way, I also don't want to ruin the trust we're starting to build.

Our beers arrive, and we clink bottles.

"I can't stay out too late. I should probably go after this and start packing," she says.

She mentioned something about a business trip earlier on the phone, but I only half caught it.

"I've got a better idea," I say, not fully in control of what was about to come out of my mouth, but it's too late now.

"What's that?"

I lean in. Way in until my lips are just brushing her earlobe. "Come upstairs with me," I whisper.

She leans back to look at me; surprise plastered all over her face.

"Don't tell me you didn't see that coming," I say with a smile.

She steals a quick glance over at the rest of the bar, probably to see if anyone was watching. They were all drinking and talking and laughing. Completely oblivious to us.

I place a finger under her chin and guide her face back toward mine. "Don't worry about them," I say. "They won't miss us."

She takes a quick swig from her bottle. The expression on her face is unreadable. She isn't angry or offended thankfully. But she isn't smiling either.

"Real talk," I say. "No more bullshit."

She nods and flashes a quick half smile. "No more bullshit," she agrees.

"I want you."

Her eyes go a little wide, but she makes no other reaction, so I continue. I stare directly into her eyes. "Do you want me?"

She doesn't answer, not at first. But she holds my gaze and doesn't break away.

"Just so we're clear," she says finally. "When you say you want me...you mean you want to fuck me?"

I smile, can't help it. She is never one to mince words. It's a big part of what attracts me to her.

I lean in closer, drop my hand to her hip. "Every man in here wants to fuck you, that I can guarantee. And probably half of the women too. That's not what I want."

She raises her eyebrow as if to say "then what do you want?"

I lean in even closer to her and lower my lips to her ear once more. Then I say, "I want to make you faint with pleasure. I want to hear my name on your lips, feel your nails on my back as I bring you to orgasm over and over again."

There. I'd said it. Let the chips fall where they may.

She looks a little shocked, slightly flushed, and so I help her along.

"Back to my question," I start. "Do you want me?"

She has to say it. I need her to say it. Flat out. Point blank. Or else this is never going to work. I'm not interested in her just going along with the motions. I want to know, I want her to be sure this is what she wants.

That I am what she wants.

She hesitates, but I don't take my eyes from hers.

"Yes," she says finally. It comes out as a half whisper, half moan.

I pause only for a split second and then reach into my pocket for my cash, slap a ten dollar bill on the table and then grab her by the arm and lead her into the building lobby toward the elevators.

I press the call button and then stand behind her, hand on her arm. I can feel her pulse quicken. "Breathe," I whisper to her.

The elevator arrives. I gently nudge her forward. Just as we get on, some guy walks up behind me. I turn and put my hand out. "Take the next one." Then I close the elevator doors.

The second the door shuts, I grab her. I pull her in close and then cover her mouth with mine. She answers back and snakes her arms up and around my neck. I push her gently against the elevator railing and then reach around her back to tug on her bra strap. It comes loose, and I pinch one of her nipples between my fingers. She gives a slight start but doesn't stop kissing me. I stop and look at her for a minute. We'll be at my floor soon, and I have to make sure of one thing before we go through with this.

"I need you to do something for me."

Again, she doesn't answer, but her eyes ask the question.

"I need you to let go. Completely. Submit to me. Give yourself to me."

I watch her breath catch. "Can you do that?"

She nods and then utters a breathless "Yes."

I bend to kiss her again, pleased for the moment. The real test, however, was yet to come.

The elevator dings, indicating that we'd reached our floor. I hold her gaze as the doors slide open. Then I place my hand firmly on the small of her back. "Walk."

We stumble into my room, pausing to kiss hungrily in the corridor. I push her backward and pin her against the door while I fish in my pocket for the key. We tumble back into the room when I finally manage to get the door open; lips locked the entire time. I'm about to slam the door until I remember that the key is still in it.

Once the door is closed, I make short work of stripping whatever clothing there is left on her and tossing it to the ground. I take a step back, slide my hand very slowly down the contour of her entire body and smile.

I feel her shiver slightly when my fingertips trail across her stomach. "You nervous?" I ask.

"No," she whispers.

"Good. I'm not going to hurt you."

Then I grab her by her wrists, hold them together, grab one of my neckties and start binding them together. Her eyes go wide, and I can't help a wicked grin.

"Well. Maybe a little."

I hook her hands onto a knob above the door and then slap the insides of her thighs until she widens her stance.

I can feel her breath quickening, her heart starting to beat faster, and it excites me.

Very slowly, I slide the belt from my pants. I stand behind her so she can't see, but the belt makes an ominous sound as it slides free from the loops.

Her muscles tense. I lightly run the belt up and down the middle of her back and then up and down each of her legs and across her ass, caressing her with it. Then I snap it just once.

She jumps.

"Safe word?"

"Poodle."

She barely gets the word out before I deliver the first blow. One wide, hard crack right in the center of her left butt cheek. The skin immediately begins to smart, and I place my hand over it and feel it getting hot.

I deliver another blow, equal in force to the other cheek. I can't tell if she's wincing or biting her lips or closing her eyes. I deliver a few more blows to her ass and outsides of her thighs before I pause. She's panting audibly now. I straighten the belt and run it lightly between her legs. It comes out slick with moisture. I smile.

"More?"

"Yes." Again, a whisper.

I start on her again with the belt, hitting harder this time and in more sensitive places. She tries hard not to let out a sound, likely thinking that in doing so, I won't think she's complaining. But now and then she lets out a whimper. I'm rock hard by this point.

When I stop, I hear her let out a long breath.

I rub my rough hand over the red of her entire ass, and she squirms. Then her body goes somewhat limp.

I unhook her wrists, and she nearly falls against me. I prop her up and then push her gently over the bed, push her over until she's bent over the side.

I can't wait.

I leave her wrists bound behind her back. Her face is in the pillow. Then I unzip, drop my pants and free my erection. I can see her pussy glistening in the moonlight. It drives me nuts and in the next second I push deep inside of her.

She lets out a loud gasp. I wait a few seconds to make sure she's adjusted, and then I grab her hips, pulling her closer toward me and begin to stroke deeply.

She moans softly at first; I can tell she's biting her lip. Then her moans gradually become louder as I fuck her faster and deeper. It eggs me on, and I lose it. It feels like heaven. Her pussy is tight and slick.

"Jesus," I mutter. I resist the urge to slap her on the ass, thinking she'd had enough punishment for one day. I adjust my stance so that I can get a smooth, downward angle, and her moans become screams.

She clenches around me and gets even wetter, and I know I've hit the sweet spot. Her hands are still bound, so she grabs at the tie instead. She has nowhere to go. She can't run. She can only stay there and take it.

And I give it to her. I give it to her good.

I'm not going to last very long like this, feels too good. I try to slow down a little, give her a chance to catch her breath. Give me a chance to catch mine. I grit my teeth to try to slow the onslaught, but I know it's coming. I feel a rapid series of muscles clenching inside of her, and I know she's close. I speed up again, fucking her a little harder. Her breathing becomes heavier, and when she pushes back on me a little, I know she's near to coming.

Hold on, I tell myself. And soon she screams and washes me with a flood of wetness, her body turning into a quivering mess.

I shove as deeply as I can go, my fingers sinking into her flesh. And then all my muscles clench up, and I empty inside of her.

She's quiet.

I let my breathing slow a little and then untie her hands. We both collapse onto the bed in a heap.

Everything goes dark.

I'm not sure what wakes me or how long I'd been out. But when I do wake, there's still a thin beam of moonlight streaming through the blinds.

She's still asleep, on her stomach and though I needed to squint a little, I can see welts beginning to pucker her skin where I'd made my marks with the belt.

I sit up and shake my head a little. Then I get up to search for the small vial of ointment I keep in my gym bag.

I walk back over to the bed, look down at her and smile. I wonder what she'd think of all this when she woke. I wonder if it was what she imagined, what she wanted.

Gently, so as not to wake her, I start to apply the ointment to the red spots on her ass.

She starts to stir when I move to the other cheek. "Try not to move," I say. She opens her eyes and looks at me, a broad grin on her face.

"What's that?" she asks softly.

"It's so you don't bruise."

She lays still, watching me as I rub the cream into her skin as gently as I possibly can. And then I cover the tube.

She turns over to lay on her back, giving a little wince when her ass hits the sheets. Her eyes lock with mine, the look on her face one of pure lust.

Slowly her legs spread, and there's no mistaking her invitation.

And then I'm on top of her, kissing her deeply. Her arms and legs wrap around me, and I rub against her like a horny dog.

I don't need to ask if she wants more.

And she doesn't need to ask me either.

I press my lips against her neck and she moans into my ear, catching the lobe between her teeth.

That drives me insane, and I move my head down to her breasts and suck her dark nipple between my lips. She arches her back and moans louder. I move to the next nipple, grazing it with my lips, my teeth and then go back to kiss her. I grab a fistful of her hair, pulling her head back.

She smiles. It's a wicked, mischievous smile. And then she grabs me by the hips, and I slide into her again.

The sound she makes when I enter her...it's everything.

She bites her lip, tries to stifle the sound.

Things I didn't notice before because I was fucking her from behind.

She claws at my back, wraps her strong thighs around my waist, and the next thing I know, I'm the one on my back.

I raise my eyebrow at her show of strength, and she just smiles. I sit up so that I can be closer to her as she moves her hips up and down on top of me. Her nipples graze my lips, and I lick at them playfully, which only seems to egg her on. She shoves me back down and starts to ride harder.

Suddenly I have to concentrate really hard on not coming. And then as if that isn't enough of a struggle, she straightens her legs and places them on either side of my head, spreads them wide open and continues to ride me.

I lift my head, and my jaw drops. She smiles again, the little minx

"You enjoying the view?" she asks.

I can't even answer; I just bite my lip. I feel like I'm going to come any second now, but I don't want to.

Not yet.

I flip her, and back onto her back she goes. She lets out a disappointed whine.

So cute.

She really thought I was going to let her win that round.

I lift her legs all the way up and bend them at the knees. "Keep them here," I instruct her and like a good girl, she keeps her legs up.

I enter again, stroking deeply. Her face contorts from the very beginning, and I know I've hit the spot. I pin her arms to the bed so that she can't move and hit that downward stroke like I'm diving into a pool.

Her moans quickly turn to screams. Her legs drop a little. "Keep those legs up. Don't get lazy." I feel her stomach muscles contract as she lifts her legs higher in the air, allowing me to penetrate her more deeply.

"Fuck you feel good," I whisper to her. "So wet...juicy." In response, she tightens her muscles around me, and I know it won't be much longer now.

I feel her come.

Hard.

Mean.

"What about you?" she whispers.

"Don't worry," I say. "I'm right behind you."

I exhale, and a thick cloud of smoke twirls up into the air. I feel her stir, somewhere in-between sleep and wakefulness. She turns over, looks at me, smiles and then reaches up to grab my cigarette from between my fingers.

She takes a long, slow drag and then exhales, her smoke twirling around and then melding with mine. I smile back at her. She scoots over and lays across my chest, her hair all over the place.

"Could use one of these right about now," she says in that sultry voice of hers. I reach over to the nightstand, take another cigarette from my pack and hand it to her.

She lays her head on my chest, and I caress her neck very lightly. We drift in and out like this for awhile.

"What time is it?" she asks after a long and satisfying silence.

"About three," I answer, not really looking because I'd checked myself not too long ago.

"I should probably go," she says quietly but makes no immediate move to leave.

"Why?"

"It's late," she replies. "And I've got a flight tomorrow."

I chuckled at this. "So?"

She smiles.

"You're not going anywhere. You're staying with me tonight."

No further discussion is needed. She laughs and says "OK."

We fall asleep again.

An hour later I wake up in a fever, and I press myself against her. It takes all of one minute for me to have her leg in the air, entering her from behind again.

I have another thoroughly satisfying orgasm, but I don't think I'm quite done.

"No more," she whimpers when I go in for another round.

I oblige and let her sleep.

14

MADISON

It's the smell of fresh coffee brewing that wakes me.

I stretch out in a bed that I realize in the next instant is not mine and for a second I panic.

Then I remember.

And smile.

No going back now, Maddy.

I get up and grab his shirt on the way out toward the smell of the coffee.

He's standing by the stove in just his underwear, and he runs and smiles when he hears me coming.

"Still here, I see," he says with a wry grin.

"Touche."

"I was half expecting to not find you here this morning."

"Can't run this time," I reply. " My legs don't fully work yet."

He slides a cup of coffee across the counter to me. Then he comes around to give me a good morning kiss. "I hate to run," he whispers. "But I have to be at work soon. You can stay here if you like."

"No. That's OK. I'll leave with you. I've got to get ready for my flight."

He nods and then disappears into his room to get dressed. I follow suit and start the scavenger hunt for my own clothes.

He reappears a little while later dressed in dark slacks and a crisp white shirt.

He seems to be struggling with his tie, so I go over to help him. He smiles down at me and then bends his head for a kiss.

Then he grabs me by the hand, and we head for the door. "I'll have my driver drop you home," he says.

In the car, he sits close to me, resting his hand on my knee and then slowly sliding it inch by inch up my dress.

I stop him when his thumb just touches the trim on my panties. "Behave," I whisper.

"Why should I?"

"Because," I say. "You'll mess up your work clothes."

"I have more at the office."

We laugh at this. Him pawing at me in the backseat of a vehicle like a horny teenager.

A minute later, we pull up in front of his office. "I can walk from here," I say. I move to get out of the car, but he catches my wrist.

"I want to ask you something," he says, his face suddenly solemn.

"What is it?"

"There's a gala. It's sort of a big deal. Something we do every year. It's in a couple of weeks." He pauses.

"And?"

"And I would love for you to accompany me."

I almost gasp. Spending the night with him was already a big step for me. Now he wanted to parade me in front of all his business partners and friends. "I don't know, Cal," I say after a minute. "That's not really my scene."

I recall the event Kim dragged me to not too long ago. It's where we first saw each other.

"I understand. I do. But I really want you there. I want you on my arm. Think about it at least?"

"I'll think about it." He seems satisfied with this and then grabs me by the back of my neck and kisses me deeply. "Call me when you get there," he whispers.

I nod and get out of the car before I end up on my back in the smooth leather seat.

He grins at me through the car window, and I poke my head through. "OK," I say. "I've thought about it. I'll go."

Then I turn to leave, having confirmed my suspicion.

I was definitely falling for this man.

The End

SAVED BY A BILLIONAIRE

AN ALPHA BILLIONAIRE ROMANCE

Madison

"There she is!" Caleb says as he comes into the bar on the ground floor of where his penthouse is.

I told him I'd meet him here. I got back into town from my business trip this morning and promised I'd grab a drink with him.

He picks me up in his strong arms and leaves a rather chaste kiss on my cheek.

I give him a look that asks the question, 'what's up?' he is usually much more full on than this.

He smiles. "You are coming up after this drink, right?"

"Wasn't planning on that, to be honest, Jones."

"Plan on it," he says with the commanding tone he can have at times.

He lets me out of his grip and I ease back onto the bar stool. It's only been a couple of days since our last little session and my ass still hurts. The smirk that flies across his handsome face lets me know he's thrilled with himself.

His lips touch my ear as he says, "Legs working right yet?"

I slap at his arm and blush. "You are a bad boy."

"Sometimes. Have you been a bad girl?" His eyes go dark and my stomach tightens.

If he knew where I really went I wonder if it would earn me more time in his bonds. More time at the end of his belt.

"I really can't go up there with you tonight. I have a lot on my mind. The business trip has me making a lot of decisions about the future which is coming at me hard and heavy. Rain check?"

"Rain check?" His hand tightens around my wrist and he looks intense. "You haven't spoken to me in two days as you said you were so busy with meetings. Is what we did something you found you don't like?"

"It's not that at all," I say and touch his cheek, running my finger over his strong jawline. "I actually found that to my liking though I never thought I would like that sort of thing."

Relief fills his face that I just realized was rather tense. "Good." He takes a deep breath. "For the last couple of days I thought you weren't real happy with that."

"And if that was the case, then what?" I take a long drink from the beer the bartender placed on the bar by me.

His fingers run over my collar bone as he whispers, "Then we wouldn't do that anymore. You're special to me, Madison. If there's anything you don't like, you don't hesitate to tell me. Honesty is key, don't you agree?"

His question about being honest has my insides squirming. What would he do if he knew the real reason I was out of town?

15

CALEB

Something isn't right with her. She's too pent up, too easily distracted. I place some money on the bar for her drink and take her by the arm. "Upstairs now. I'm not taking no for an answer."

I haul her up and she looks at me with a frown. "I don't know how good company I'll be. I have to warn you. I'm tired and a little pissy."

"I can fix that." My fingers I press on the small of her back and the mere touch of her is making me hard.

I have to get her upstairs and undressed.

She turns to me after we get in the elevator. "So when do I get my real hello kiss?" she asks with a grin.

"There she is, my naughty little minx."

I run my arms around her and press her back to the wall. Around my neck her arms go and my mouth takes hers in a hard kiss. Her tongue runs into my mouth and she twirls her tongue with mine.

The elevator door opens and we step out into my apartment without letting each other go. I kick my shoes off and pull her up off the floor into my arms. Her heels hit the floor as she kicks them off.

There's no need to ask her if she wants this. The way she's kissing me and groping at my shirt tells me she does.

We fall on top of the bed and I grind my hard cock against her soft core and she groans.

Her hands move to unbutton my slacks and I stop her. I pull away from her and smile.

"Who is in charge here?"

She takes in a deep breath. "You."

I wink and wrestle with her tight skirt to get it off. Her shirt she starts to unbutton and I take her hand in mine.

"No."

She smiles and moves her hands back.

I get her completely naked then lie her back and hold her hands over her head.

"Aren't you going to get undressed?"

I lift my head and look at her. "Shh. Just lie back and let me play."

A frustrated sigh she makes and I smack her thigh as I go back to sucking on her juicy tit that I find I missed way too much.

She wiggles her ass on the bed and I give her another hard smack on her thigh. She stills then says, "Again."

I smile at her and smack her again. She groans and my dick goes all the way to beyond hard.

Moving my mouth from her tit, I stand and drop my pants and pull my shirt off over my head. "Look what you've done to me," I say as I pull her up by her hand and run it over my erection.

She peers up at me and licks her lips. Her eyes ask me if she can and I give her a nod.

I watch as she runs her hands up and down my girth and nearly pass out as her lips run over the large head. "Damn it, baby!"

She moans as she runs her mouth all the way down it. She hesitates as it touches the back of her throat then pushes it further and moans more as she does. I join her in the moaning as it feels fucking fantastic.

Her hands move over my dick as she pulls her mouth back up it, never leaving any of it exposed. In and out and up and down she pulls me with her mouth and hands and it's not long before I'm about to let go.

But I can't do that just yet.

Tangling my hands into her long blonde hair, I pull her back.

"My turn."

She smiles and moves back on the bed, knees bent and ready for me.

Moving in steady and slow. I kiss the inside of her thighs as I make my way up her body.

She arches up and squeals as my lips touch her throbbing clit.

Gripping her ass cheeks in each hand I pull her up to me and feast on her.

She's already soaking wet, but I intend on make her even wetter.

Slowly I torture her with my tongue. Just when I feel she's about to let go, I leave her clit and run my tongue slowly down through her folds.

She's impatient and needs to learn how to let me take my time with her.

Her hands run over my head and through my hair as she gently presses me to finish her. "Please, Cal," she groans.

She did say please.

My tongue darts back to her clit and I suck on it hard and she begins her descent, arching and moaning like there's no tomorrow.

My dick is as hard as it can get and I know when I push it inside her I'm going to have to focus not to join her already.

I ease up her body and kiss her as I go up. It gives her body time to slow the pulses it's making.

Our eyes meet as I rise up over her and I smile and give her a wink. "Hi."

The blue of her eyes is deep and dark with desire and she grabs the back of my neck and pulls me into a hard kiss.

Her tongue moves all over my mouth and her need for me is consuming her.

This definitely will not take long.

I press my rock hard cock into her wet and slippery slope and we both groan as I enter and fill her.

A moment I wait to allow her to accommodate my girth then she arches up and wraps her legs around me.

Her kiss is hungry and I know she wants this hard and fast.

Who am I to deny the poor girl?

Making hard thrusts, I feel her breath push up into her mouth with each one.

It's taking everything I have not to come and when she starts convulsing around me, it's over.

I tense and my body lets it all out.

She moans and I grunt as we come undone together.

Madison

My eyes open and it would probably be best for me to leave before Caleb wakes up. The man is insatiable and kept waking me up after short periods of sleep to have a little bit more.

I'm not complaining, but I am really tired.

I squirm out of his arms and his eyes fly open. "Where do you think you're going?"

Uh, oh!

"I thought you might sleep better if I got out of your bed and let you stretch out."

He takes my hands and pulls me back to him. "I sleep better with you in my bed. Now lay back down and sleep, you silly girl."

I'm not a silly girl, anything but that. I'd rather not get into why I can't sleep with him so I snuggle back into his warm arms and settle back in.

The reason I had to go on the supposed business meeting keeps running through my head.

It was business, but it was family business. My mother died several years ago and my father never was a real winner and became less of one after she passed away from cancer.

He got into running drugs for the local mafia and a few years ago he was caught bringing a bunch of them across the border and into Texas.

He was caught at a check point and promptly sent to jail and then prison. He's getting out soon. That's ending up as really bad news for me.

He wants me to get in touch with his old boss.

Talking to men in the Mafia is not my idea of fun or safe. I don't plan on doing that even though my father has threatened to ruin my music label business.

It was he who got me kicked out of nursing school when he made me steal pharmaceuticals from the hospital I was training in. I was lucky they merely kicked me out instead of pressing charges on me.

I was caught before I left the hospital so they didn't lose any of their drugs. I guess that's why they let me off so easy.

My father plans on staying with me in my tiny apartment though I told him there could be no drugs or alcohol as he has addictions to both.

Truth be told, I don't want to deal with him at all, but when the man puts his mind to something like fucking up the career I've managed to make for myself, well, let's just say he should be taken seriously.

Caleb is bound to feel differently about me once my father arrives. He is a style cramper, extraordinaire.

I cannot see what my mother ever saw in the man.

The rest of the night is going to be a long one as I am now trapped like a rat here in Caleb's arms.

There could be worse traps though.

16

CALEB

"How about lunch?" I ask Madison over my cell as I look out the window of my office and reminisce about last night.

She was hot, hot, hot. It was obvious she missed me. I know I missed her.

The girl has gotten way up underneath my skin.

"Can't. Too much work. Sorry."

"You have to eat. Let me bring something to you?"

"No!" Her tone is sharp, and the word comes out too shrill.

"Who do you have over there you don't want me to know about?" I tap my desk top with my fingertips.

Something is not right with her.

"At this moment it's only me. Don't think like that, Jones."

"Alright, I guess I can give you the time you need to straighten out your work shit. But you're staying the night with me."

"No," she says and sighs. "I really need to stay at my place tonight. Every night really. This staying with you is getting out of hand. Don't you agree?"

"Not even a little, Madison. What's up with you?"

"Nothing is up with me. Damn! I have shit to do, Cal. That's all. I'll talk to you later. I have to go. I have a call I need to make and you're slowing me down today."

"Slowing you down? Wow! Okay, bye."

I end the call and want to throw the phone against a wall. The chick is making me so damn mad!

Something is up and I will get to the bottom of it. And it will be tonight whether she likes it or not!

17

MADISON

Just as I walk out of my office I see Caleb leaning up against the brick wall outside of it, a smoking cigarette in between his fingers which he flicks away once he sees me.

I'm instantly aroused, but also pissed as he doesn't listen to me, obviously. "Stalk much?" I say between clenched teeth.

I'm immediately sorry as his handsome face looks like I just slapped him. "We need to talk. You need to tell me what's wrong. I know there's something and you just need to get it off your chest."

I walk quickly and he stays right by my side. "There's nothing. It's just business has me stressed out."

"Bull shit! I'm not buying that, Madison. Let's stop up here at this bar. We can have a drink and a cigarette and you can chill and tell me what has crawled up your ass."

I stop and look at him. Maybe I should tell him that my asshole father is basically blackmailing me into having to take him in.

Caleb's tie is dark blue and his suit is black and expensive as hell. Everything about him screams Harvard and filthy rich. My father would have a field day digging something up to hold over Caleb's head to get as much of his money as he could.

For Caleb's own protection I need to end this before my father gets here and ruins what's left of my life.

"I'd rather not do this on the street, Cal. Call me later and we can talk over the phone." I try to walk away but his hand squeezes my wrist.

"No. You're going to come home with me. There's something you're hiding and I want to know what it is. Shit! I can probably help you out of whatever it is that's got you acting so crazy."

Maybe he could. Maybe I should tell him.

Searching his blue eyes for the answer I'm startled as my cell phone rings. I grab it out of my coat pocket and see the area code in Texas.

It's my father calling from prison. I can't answer it in front of Caleb.

I press the button to ignore the call and Caleb's eyes about pop out of his head.

"Who the hell was that, Madison?"

"I have no idea. Sales people have been calling me left and right."

"You're lying! I can tell. Your eyes go everywhere but to mine and I know you're keeping something from me."

Pulling me along. I can see his car and driver out of the corner of my eye. It pulled up just a little ways in front of us and Caleb is pulling me towards it.

"We're going home!"

"That's not my home, Caleb. Stop! You can't make me go."

It doesn't make him stop dragging me along behind him. The driver gets out and holds the car door open and Caleb slides me in and slides right in beside me.

"Take us home," he tells the driver.

His voice is low and controlled and a lot scary. "Your secrets aside, have you forgotten who you belong to?"

Now I'm just pissed.

"Just because we've fucked doesn't mean I belong to you."

"Is that how you think about what we've done together? Because that is one ugly way of looking at it."

"What we've done is totally fucking. Come on! You fucking tied my ass up and beat me with your leather belt. That's fucking, Caleb!"

"I did not beat you, Madison. Please, don't even say that. And you told me you liked it."

"Who the hell likes to get their ass beat?"

The look on his face lets me know I'm starting to get him to think differently of me. That's exactly what I need him to do. He needs to think I'm not the girl he thought I was.

I'm not the girl for him.

18

CALEB

She may as well have punched me in the stomach. "Stop that." I manage to get to come out of my mouth.

She shakes her head. "I won't."

Something isn't right. I take her by the back of her neck and pull her to me quickly so she can't stop me.

I take her mouth in a hard kiss and her body tenses then she relaxes against mine. No matter what is happening in her head, her body knows what it wants and it wants me.

Her arms wrap around me and I run mine around her. I feel the car stop and open my eyes to see we're in front of my building.

The driver opens my door and I pull my mouth from hers and grab her hand, pulling her along with me.

I have to get her ass upstairs and naked and back in my bed. Then she'll calm down and I'll get her to confide in me what it is that's making her act this way.

Straight to the elevator I take her and as soon as the doors close I pull her to me and kiss her again. Her body's hot against mine and I think I feel tears running down her cheeks.

I don't stop my kiss to find out though. I need to get her inside my penthouse.

The elevator stops and I take her into the living room and start to drag her clothes off. By the time we get to the bedroom I have her how I want her, naked and wet for me.

Her mouth is hot and her tongue runs over every inch of my mouth, seemingly searching for something.

I run my hand between us and find her wet and ready to go. With a strong push I shove her down on the bed and hurry to undress myself as she looks all over my body.

I can't be rough. I have to let her know how much she really means to me.

19

MADISON

I let myself really take Caleb in. His body is magnificent and this will be the last time I ever see it.

After this I will hurt him so bad he has no choice but to end things with me. But one last time I need to feel him before I give him up for his own protection.

The way his muscles ripple across his chest is a thing of beauty and I may miss that the most.

Not everyone has a body like his. Not that I'll be finding anyone else. My father will find a way to pilfer from any man I become involved with.

A relationship just isn't on the cards for me.

Unless my father got sent away again.

Caleb moves his body over mine and his eyes show a lot of concern in the deep blue depths.

Man, I'm going to miss looking into his eyes.

This one last time I'll give him all of me. He deserves that. He doesn't deserve the hurt I'll have to give him, but it's what's best for him.

I stop breathing as he presses his body to mine. The heat between us is phenomenal.

Gently he presses his erection into me and I want to cry with how right it feels. Everything about him says home to me.

I pull his face in to kiss me as I don't want him to see the tears which are about to run down my face.

His kiss is gentle too. The way he's handling my body is soft and dare I say, loving.

A slow, deep rhythm he makes as he moves in and out of me. His body tight to mine everywhere else as he keeps me closed in.

I run my hands over his back and try to memorize each and every corded muscle. I'll have to remember him.

The tears flow on their own as my mind knows what my body doesn't. There will be no more of this.

I arch up to him and he grinds against me, driving his thick cock in deeper.

His lips leave mine and go to my neck to nip and suck at it. He murmurs near my ear, "Baby, you feel like Heaven."

Tingles run through me with his words and I moan.

Fingertips trail down my arm then my side, sending chills throughout my body.

Back to my mouth his sweet lips come and I welcome him in.

Hot, slow kisses he gives me. I never want this to end, but my body is beginning to feel the familiar feeling of an orgasm.

The wave is building, and he grinds into me a little harder, a little deeper and his kiss goes deeper as well.

This is killing me because this has to be what love feels like.

And I have to let it go.

20

CALEB

My heart physically hurts. Madison has something weighing so heavy on her she's talked in her sleep most of the night.

I made love to her then let her fall asleep in my arms.

Even though her body reacted so well, she never stopped crying.

I didn't let on that I realized she was crying. She was trying hard to hide the fact that tears were continuously running down her cheeks.

Maybe in the morning she'll feel safe enough with me to tell me her problems.

For tonight I can only guess and I'm probably guessing much worse things than it actually is.

It's run through my mind that she has a husband somewhere. Maybe a whole family, kids and all.

Perhaps something else, like she had a reason for quitting the nursing school. Maybe she had an affair with a doctor who wants her back. Maybe she did something accidentally horrible to a patient, and the family is harassing her.

That's what it seems like, that she feels very harassed.

I know I can be overbearing and a bit of a control freak. I'm not perfect.

I just know what I'm asking of her is not harassing her. It's someone else.

The phone call she didn't answer has me worried too.

Who would be calling her that she didn't want to talk to, at least not in front of me?

I run my fingers over her soft, bare skin and she shivers a little.

Pulling the blanket up to cover her better I pull her tighter against me.

This feels like it's supposed to be.

I wonder if this is it. The real deal. This feels like love to me.

21

MADISON

Bacon fills my senses, and the sunlight makes me slam my lids shut as soon as I open them.

Caleb's voice creeps into the bedroom from the kitchen. "What do you mean I have to be there? I told you I want to take the day off to deal with some important things I have going on. So just explain to them that I agree with you and the rest of the partners."

What does he have to deal with today I wonder?

My clothes are all in the living room. I'd like just once to be able to find my clothes and put them back on without making a scavenger hunt for them.

His voice wafts in again. "Fine, Shit! Fuck! I'll be there."

Wrapping the sheet around me I walk out to find Caleb picking up my clothes. He spins around with them and his face is red.

His expression softens quickly, and he comes to me. "Good morning, baby."

I'm picked up into his arms and his mouth is on mine as he takes me back to the bedroom. "I really have to go, Cal."

"I know. I do too. I had other plans for us today, but the damn partners need me."

I breathe a sigh of relief that he won't be fighting me about leaving.

I have a little more time before I have to break him.

He's already dressed, the early riser he is. I pull on my clothes and know I have to go by my apartment to get ready for work.

"See you later," I say as I step into my last shoe.

"You're letting my driver take you home."

"I can grab a cab." I move towards the door.

"No. You will take my car and my driver will take you home. I will grab a cab and go to my office."

"That's too much trouble. Really, I can catch a cab."

"Fuck!" His arms fly into the air. "You're taking the car. End of discussion!"

"Fine!" I shut up and make my way out of the bedroom.

Just as I reach the elevator I feel his hand on my shoulder and he spins me around.

His arms go around me and his kiss melts me to him.

Finally, he pulls his lips off mine, leaving them pulsing.

"Have a good day, baby. See you back here tonight." He slips a gold key into my hand.

The key to his apartment. I look up and nearly cry, but somehow manage to hold it all back. "A key?"

He folds his hands over mine to close it in my grasp. "I want you to feel free to come and go as you please. Bring some clothes and things to make yourself more comfortable around here."

I shake my head and know I can't do this. "Caleb, this is a nice gesture but I suppose it's time to let you in on the truth."

I try to hand him the key back but he won't take it. I place it on the tall table near me and try to move past him.

"Just tell me." He pulls me back to him.

"This isn't working."

"It's not, huh? The way you reacted to me last night tells me there's something more to it than this just isn't working."

"There's no more to it than that. You're a distraction from what I really want. I have to put all my focus on my business right now. A relationship isn't a thing I can have right now. Maybe never. And you aren't really my type anyway."

His eyes grow narrow and the blue in them goes to a new level of deep.

He releases my arm and shakes his head. "You thought this was a relationship?" He turns and laughs. "I was giving you a key only so you would be more readily available to me, nothing more than that. A sweet piece of ass is all you are to me."

Though I know this is exactly what would happen if I made him feel he was nothing to me, it still hurts like I never imagined it would.

"Then you shouldn't mind that we don't see each other anymore. Nice knowing you, Jones." I walk away and stay strong, keeping a stiff upper lip.

All the way to the car I keep it together. It's a blessing Caleb is letting me take this home. I manage to choke out my address before silent sobs rack my chest.

If this is the right thing to do why in the hell does it hurt so fucking bad?

22

CALEB

"You look like hell," Brad tells me as he walks into my office.

"Thanks." I push back from my desk and get up, grabbing my jacket off the back of the chair. "I guess it's time to get to the conference room for the important call I had to be here for."

He claps his hand on my back as we walk out. "Is this about that chick you've been hanging out with?"

"Nope." I keep walking and not talking.

I've yet to talk about Madison with any of my friends and now that it's over I see no reason to start now.

"Maybe after the conference we can go get a drink, maybe some dinner." Brad pulls the glass door open and I see the rest of the partners gathered around the conference table.

This should be a damn great day!

23

MADISON

A week has passed since I left Caleb's penthouse. My heart has never felt this much pain. I keep thinking every night that the next morning it won't hurt so much, but it does.

Even more than the night before it seems.

I want to call Caleb and see if he's okay.

This is the date of the big gala he invited me to. I won't be going to that now. I won't be on his strong arm, the envy of so many women.

No, I'll be home, biding my time until my father shows his face and begins the torment that is sure to come along with the way he lives.

I still haven't contacted his old boss and the phone calls from the prison stopped a couple of days ago.

I don't know why they stopped. I hope my father found someone else to live with when he's released.

A girl can dream, can't she?

The door opens, making a chime sound so I go to the reception area to see who's here as Nicole, my receptionist is on her lunch break.

A man stands holding a giant bouquet of red roses. He offers me a wide smile and hands me an envelope. "Here you go, Madison. And may I say you are every bit as beautiful as Mr. Jones said you were."

I take the envelope from his outstretched hand and gesture for him to place the monster crystal vase full of flowers on a table in the reception area.

"Thank you, that's sweet of you to say."

The young man bows for some odd reason and leaves.

I open the envelope and pull out the card.

At some time or another the crazy man took a selfie of him and me as I slept in his arms. The picture is on the outside of the card. I open it to find only a few words printed inside – **Hurt-Jerk-Forgive Me-Come with me to the Gala-** *PLEASE XXOO*

The chime goes off again, and another man walks in holding a large white box. "You have to be Madison. Oh my, Mr. Jones wasn't kidding when he said you were gorgeous!"

I smile and gesture for him to put the box on the receptionist's desk. "What do we have here?"

He pulls the top off, revealing a magnificent and horribly expensive black dress with dark blue accents.

"You will be to die for in this, if I may say so." The man spins on his heel and leaves without another word.

I pull the dress from the box and hold it out in front of me. Slim lines show me this will fit me much like a glove. I peer into the box to find a nice pair of heels to go with it.

Just as I start thinking about the jewelry I have to wear with it, the door chimes again and in walks another young man. He has a black box and a smile on his face.

"Wow! What a knock out, just like the boss said."

"You work for Mr. Jones," I ask.

"I keep his car washed and detailed at all times. I'm Jeff. I'm also his nephew. It's real nice to meet you, Madison. I hope we see you around a lot. You know, family gatherings and stuff like that. Christmas is just around the corner."

I sigh and say, "Your uncle and I aren't like that, Jeff. But that's a really nice thing to say."

"We'll see," he says then leaves.

I can't stop myself and say, "I know, unfortunately. But I would be a real bitch not to go with him to this thing. I can do that much for the man."

I pick up my phone and tap in a text to him. -**Pick me up at 8 and thanks for the things, they're all beautiful.**

My phone dings right back with a text from him -**YOU ARE BEAUTIFUL!!! I will be there and thank you XXOO.**

This is so not smart for my poor heart, but I can't let him go alone.

Tomorrow I'll break it all off again. There should be time before my father arrives, which could be any time now.

At least I'll be at the gala tonight. And with Caleb.

My heart just skipped a beat for some odd reason.

This has to be what love feels like.

Too bad I can't have that in my life.

24

CALEB

"I know I've kept her a secret, Mom. I can't believe Jeff told his mother. Dang!"

"Tomorrow, dinner, promise me," Mom says with a 'not taking no for an answer' attitude in her high voice.

"If she agrees I'll definitely bring her. But don't count on it for sure until I talk to you tomorrow. She still has something she hasn't let me in on. I know she's doing this as a social favor. Well, she might love me too. I mean I hope she thinks about me like I do her."

"You love her. Don't you, son?"

"I do."

The words actually coming out of my mouth numb my brain.

Tonight has to be magical to make her see we are meant to be together.

"Gotta go, Mom. It's time for me to leave."

"Love you, Caleb."

"Love you, Mom."

I end the call and take the little black box with the not so little engagement ring in it. A little silent prayer I give and head out to the car.

Madison

I have to admit the dress is fabulous and the heels even feel fantastic. I've made a pact with myself not to look up the designers and find out how much he paid for this stuff.

I know I would shit if I knew how much the things I'm wearing cost.

They'll all go back tomorrow.

I'll give myself this evening though. I need it. I miss Caleb more than I thought possible. One little dose of him should get me over the hump.

A deep breath I take then head out to meet his car. I said to be here at eight and his driver is always punctual. I didn't give him my apartment number so he can't come up and surprise me.

I pass the mirror near my door and stop to admire how the jewels sparkle and think this is as close to looking like a princess I'll ever get.

The elevator takes me down to the ground floor and I walk out looking for the car.

"Hey! Is that you, Maddy?" a man asks.

I turn to find my father standing behind me. A brown, paper sack in one hand and a large bottle of beer in the other.

"What are you doing here?"

He comes towards me with his arms open. "Aren't you glad to see your daddy, pumpkin?"

"I've got somewhere to be. If you can't tell by my dress. You'll have to go somewhere else until tomorrow." I step back as he comes closer.

"No!" he shouts then shakes his head and stops himself. "Maddy, just let me into your apartment. I need to get some things going and I need a place to set up my business. If you know what I'm saying, baby girl?"

"Yeah, you need a place to sell drugs out of. That is not happening. What's in the bag?"

"A little of this and a little of that." He shakes the bag as if its enticing me. "You might want a little somethin' somethin' for your party tonight. A little blow maybe. It'll help you stay up late and get your party on."

My stomach twists as this is my father offering me drugs after all. I shake my head and say, "You disgust me. Find somewhere else to do your shit. My place is off limits." I turn on my heel and leave.

The car isn't here yet and I look up and down the street to see if it's anywhere near here. I need to leave now.

My arms is wrenched behind my back and my father is pushing me back to my building. "You are going to let me in. If you do what I say I might not beat the shit out of you. So help me, Maddy. I will not tolerate disrespect."

"Dad! Stop!" He pushes me hard and I fall to the ground.

My present attire doesn't make protecting myself very easy.

The dress is tight and makes getting up nearly impossible.

My father grabs a handful of my hair and pulls me up off the side-walk. "Get your ass inside. There will be no party for you!"

For the love of God, why didn't I tell Caleb my apartment number?

"Look, stop! Please!" I shout.

Only a few people are out and one stops. "Hey! Let her go!" a lady calls out.

My father turns and I fly as he holds my hair tight. "Mind your business, bitch!"

"It's okay, lady," I say. "Please don't get involved. He might hurt you."

She shakes her head and walks away.

"I will hurt you, bitch. Keep walking!" My father turns back towards the building and pulls me along as I try not to fall as he has me walking backwards as he pulls my hair.

"Please, just let me go. I'll take you inside. I swear. Just let me go!"

The brick wall of my building finds me quickly as he throws me up against it. He's let go of my hair but his fist is about to connect with my face and all I can do is brace myself for the punch.

25

CALEB

What the fuck!

I jump out of the car and race to stop some man from punching the love of my life.

The way Madison is just waiting for the punch has my mind reeling. She knocked a big ass man out before, so why's she going to let this old guy hit her?

"Hey, fucker!" I shout but the man is so focused on Madison he doesn't turn back.

I grab his balled up fist as he draws it back and he finally looks at me.

"Fuck off! This is none of your concern! This is between me and my daughter."

"This is your father?" I ask in disbelief.

Madison's eyes were squeezed shut as she prepared to take the punch. She opens them and relief fills her beautiful face. "Caleb! Thank God!"

I twist the man's hand and pull it behind his back and press him to the wall he had Madison up against. "Get behind me, Madison," I order.

She moves behind me as I hold her father to the wall. Sirens fill the air as someone must have seen what he was doing and called the police.

"You, okay, baby?" I ask her as I feel her arms go around me from behind.

"I am now."

She buries her head against my back and I can feel her body shaking.

I want to beat the living shit out of this man. But since the cops are coming I'll keep my temper.

"Maddy, I will fuck you up once this prick lets me go!"

Oh hell no!

I pull him back and slam him back against the bricks. "Shut the fuck up! You'll never lay a hand on your daughter again, you piece of shit!"

She tightens her arms around me and whispers, "Thank you, Caleb."

In a flurry of dark blue, several policemen swarm around us and one takes over my hold on her father.

"What's going on here?" one of the policemen ask.

Madison's father answers, "This bitch is my daughter and she was being a disobedient little shit. I was merely taking her back up to our apartment. I didn't hurt her. Tell them, honey."

He looks at her as the officer turns him to face us. I pull her into my arms and she buries her face in my chest. "He doesn't live with me," she says. "He's fresh out of prison and if you check that bag in his hand you should find enough shit to put him back there."

On the ground he goes as the cops cuff him and take the bag and open it. "Jackpot!" one of the officers shouts. "Thanks for the tip, honey."

I hug her close. "I'm so sorry this happened. We were just a little late. It will never happen again."

"You wanna file assault charges miss?" the head officer asks her.

"She does," I answer.

Her father shouts from his place on the ground. "Shut the fuck up, whoever you are. Don't listen to him, he's nobody."

"Tell them," I tell Madison as I turn her to face the officer.

"I want to press charges sir. He's my father and I love him as such, but he is an awful man and really shouldn't be let loose on the streets. I want to prosecute him to the fullest extent of the law."

I squeeze her shoulders and pull her back to me. "That's my girl." I kiss the side of her head.

"She's my girl," her father snaps.

An officer picks him up and pushes him towards a waiting police cruiser. "No more of that crap. I'm putting you in the car where you can no longer hurt that girl."

With a loud yell that sounds like its out of a horror movie her father shouts, "I will get you for this Madison! Mark my words, they can't keep me locked up forever, you little bitch!"

I pull her close to me. "Can I take her up to her apartment?" I ask one of the officers.

He nods. "One of us will come up and get a full statement and let her sign the document about the assault charges. What's the apartment number?"

"726," she says and I take her away from the terrible scene.

"Is that what had you acting so crazy?" I ask as I lead her inside.

Her green eyes shine with tears as she looks up at me. "You saw the man. If he knew you and I were seeing each other he'd have blackmailed you for money for the rest of his life. I couldn't do that to you. I couldn't bring that into your life."

As we enter the elevator I kiss her forehead. "You should've told me and let me deal with that. I do know a thing or two about the law. A Harvard grad if you will recall. He must have been threatening you from prison."

She nods. "He was. He said I had to let him live with me. His plan was to sell drugs out of my apartment."

"I see." My heart pounds hard in my chest as all I really want to do is go kill the bastard. "Well, that's over."

"Thank you, Caleb. I don't know what I would've done if I hadn't accepted your invitation. He'd have gotten inside and then I'd never have gotten out of this thing. I'll get cleaned back up and after I talk to the officer we can get on the way to the gala."

"We will do no such thing. You've been through a traumatic experience, Madison. Give yourself a little while to mentally deal with that."

We come to her door and walk inside. The apartment is minuscule and though clean and furnished nicely, it's nearly suffocating in here, it's so small.

26

MADISON

I feel like I'm in shock or something as I wash the make-up off my face and look into the mirror. I have a scratch on my left cheek from where my father pushed me up against the brick wall. My forehead is red where it bumped the wall.

The bathroom door opens and Caleb comes inside with a pair of sweats. "Put these on and after you talk to the cops I'm taking you home with me."

"You don't have to, Cal. I'll be fine. He's not getting out anytime soon."

His finger touches my chin and his voice is firm. "I'm taking you home. End of discussion."

No use arguing with him. He will get his way in the end and I'm exhausted anyway.

"Okay, thank you."

Gently he runs his finger tip over the scratch on my cheek. "Fucking bastard," he mutters. "Did he do this to you a lot as a kid?"

"My mother ran interference. She got more beatings than I did. Only because she placed herself between us."

He pulls me into his arms and sighs. "I wish you would've let me in on that part of your life, baby. I never would've done what I did to you."

I press my hand to his chest so he lets me go a little and I can look him in his eyes. "Caleb, I swear to you that I liked that. I didn't think of it like a punishment. It was exciting and I don't want you to think anything different. My father beat me. It wasn't anywhere near what we did."

"You sure?" he asks with concern etched on his handsome face.

I nod and cup the back of his neck with my hand and pull him towards me. "Now how about you give me a kiss as I have missed you like I could never have imagined."

"Good. Never leave me out of things again. I never want this to happen again."

I nod and pull him to me.

His lips touch mine and fire rips through me with the intense emotions I have.

Slow swirls he makes with his tongue around mine and I know without a doubt things will be okay again.

27

CALEB

Though nothing went as planned, I finally have Madison back home and snuggled up in bed. I'm bringing her a glass of wine and a little something else.

"Hey," she says as I come into the bedroom.

She sits up and props a few pillows behind her back. I hand her the glass and sit down next to her on the bed.

She takes a sip then sets the glass down and pulls at the lapels of my jacket. "Get undressed and come to bed with me."

"One thing first," I say and pull the little black box from my pocket.

She looks at the box in my hand and her hand goes to her mouth. She shakes her head in what I hope is just disbelief and not her answer.

I open the top and her eyes go wide. Then she looks at me.

"I'm tired of playing games, Madison. I knew it from the moment I laid eyes on you that you were the one. Will you please make me the happiest man in the world and become my wife?"

It takes her a small eternity to answer me and my hands are on the verge of shaking.

She clears her throat and I can tell her answer was taking so long because she couldn't talk.

"Yes," she manages to get out before the tears start to fall.

I place the ring on her finger and kiss behind her ear. "Thank you. I love you, Madison."

Her arms go around me and she holds me to her tight. "I love you too, Caleb."

Looks like all's well that ends well.

The End

Did you like this book? Then you'll LOVE Dangerous Desire.

From the first moment, Winter Mai had me hooked.
Her beauty, her will to survive...
But she hates me—and with good reason.
My best friend, my brother, murdered her sister and almost killed Winter, too.
She doesn't know about the sleepless nights I spent silently begging her to live...
And now, all these years later, she's right in front of me, and in the arms of a man I know to be a violent and dangerous criminal.
I won't let anything hurt her. I owe her...
...and I'm desperately—achingly—in love with her.
Will she ever forgive me?
Her face and her body haunt my dreams, and I won't be happy until Winter is my arms, my life, and my bed...

Start Reading Dangerous Desire NOW!

https://books2read.com/u/bOAL7Q

SNEAK PEEK - CHAPTER 1

Start Reading Dangerous Desire NOW!

https://books2read.com/u/bOAL7Q

Portland Harbor, Oregon

As usual, it was the fireworks that triggered her. The sound of the *pop-pop-pop-pop-pop* in the night sky above the harbor was endless, and although Winter tried all the techniques the counselor had taught her, she still ended up trembling underneath the bunk in her bedroom.

She squeezed her eyes shut and tried to visualize her happy place, playing with her childhood dog, Crunchy, in the wheat fields of her youth in Kokomo, Indiana. Those few years when her father was stationed at that military base were the happiest of Winter's life.

Pop-pop-pop-pop-pop. It's just fireworks, that is all it is...

Blood. Screaming. Terror. An ordinary Saturday afternoon shopping with her sister at the mall...

Pop-pop-pop-pop-pop.

She hears a strange keening sound, like a wounded animal, except the sound is coming from *her,* and she stuffs her hands into her own mouth to stop herself. Anyone close by would wonder why she was screaming, and out here on her tiny houseboat in Portland Harbor, a million miles away from where it had happened, they might come to help her.

The last thing she needed now were strangers on her boat, in her home. Her skin itched at the thought of it.

Finally, just after one a.m. the fireworks ended, and Winter crawled out panting from under the bunk. She sat with her knees drawn up to her chest and took several deep breaths. Her chest felt fluttery, her psyche fragile, and she let a few hot tears fall down her cheeks before she rebuked herself.

You're twenty-seven years old, Winter Mai. You're an adult. Fireworks are just that. Fireworks.

She scrambled to her feet—too quickly—and grabbed the edge of the bunk as she swayed, dizzy. Her back was aching from being scrunched up beneath the bunk, and she stretched it out with a couple of yoga moves, pretending to herself that she was relaxing.

In reality, her ears were tuned, ready for more. Fear was turning into anger. Who the hell was letting off fireworks? It was early November; Thanksgiving still three weeks away. It wasn't an election year nor had any other big event occurred.

Just some assholes celebrating a goddamned birthday or something, and fuck everyone else's peace, Winter thought angrily now. That irritation propelled her out onto her deck to seek out the perpetrator despite her frazzled nerves.

The culprit wasn't difficult to spot. The vast yacht that was moored in the harbor had arrived two days ago and was now jam-packed with people. A party. A thick pall of smoke hung about it, and Winter could still see small fireworks being set off from it. *Assholes.*

To make herself feel better, she gave it the finger with both hands and stomped back inside.

Winter shut her door and sunk down into her ancient but comfortable sofa, glancing at the clock. She had a nine o'clock appointment in the morning to give a piano lesson to one of her students, so sleep was definitely the best idea now... except she knew it wouldn't come. Truthfully, her constant nightmares prevented her from getting any solid sleep nowadays, and it was only when she took a sleeping pill that she got any rest at all.

But they made her feel so crappy the next day... *no*. She got up and went to take a shower. Even in the cold of an Oregon winter, she was sweating and clammy from the terror of the fireworks. She stripped off and studied herself in the floor-length mirror. She could do with gaining a couple of pounds; her slight frame the result from a lack of appetite and not being able to afford much food. All her money, all the awarded compensation from the... 'thing'... had gone into buying this houseboat; now she had to live paycheck-to-paycheck from the small amount of money she earned as a freelance piano tutor.

That didn't matter, she thought now. *I don't need money. I just want peace...* and for most of the time, that's what this little haven in Portland gave her. She didn't see many people—didn't *want* to see anyone —except for the few students she had, and she was very lucky to have them.

Winding her long dark hair up into a bun, Winter stepped into the shower. The daughter of a Chinese-American father and a Dutch mother, she was the youngest of three sisters. Her two older siblings, Summer and Autumn, were older by two and four years respectively, the latter a famed celebrity chef now back in New York. Summer had been with Winter when the shooting happened.

Winter survived, although badly injured. *Summer...*

Summer didn't make it.

Winter stood under the water until it turned cold, but she still felt like her skin was on fire. She pressed her hands to the scars across her chest and stomach. The bullets had missed her major organs and arteries, unbelievably so, considering she had been shot six times, but Summer hadn't been so lucky.

Stop it. Winter shook herself, cranking off the shower faucet and stepping, shivering now, out of the shower. She dried herself quickly and dressed in jeans and a sweater, tugging on thick socks and her sneakers.

After busying herself with making a cup of tea, Winter stepped out onto her houseboat deck. It was bitingly cold, but that's what she wanted—the cool air on her skin. She sat down on the small love seat and sipped her fragrant tea. While watching the fete slowly break up and partygoers boisterously leaving the yacht, she could see them thanking a tall man, dark and exquisitely dressed in a dark grey suit and a blue shirt. She guessed him to be in his forties, carrying an athletic build with strong legs and broad shoulders. His hair was cut short, and his face was handsome, as chiseled as a Roman God. He was clearly the owner of the yacht, and Winter wondered who he was.

Wondering the name of the man I should hate for putting me through this night. She knew she was scowling, but she didn't care; she even hoped he would see her and realize he had upset her. Winter hoped some of the other people who lived here would be out of their homes as well, giving him hell for keeping them awake.

But she guessed that none of them likely react to fireworks the way she does. She sighed. She hated this time of year; so many noisy holidays that could provoke more nights like this: Thanksgiving, Christmas, New Year. Along with July 4th, they were her least favorite days of the year, but at least she could expect them—prepare. Noise cancelling headphones and Pearl Jam at full blast. When she could afford it, she would drive to a motel out in the middle of nowhere on July 4th just to avoid all the fireworks and celebrations.

But when they were unexpected, like tonight, she had no time to prepare. *Fuck...* Winter knew she would be upset for days now, her equilibrium rocked. She sighed and closed her eyes. Another sleepless night was on its way unless she gave in to that little bottle of pills on her bathroom sink.

Raziel Ganz said goodbye to the last of his guests and made his way back up to the now-darkened party deck. For the last hour or so, he'd been waiting to be alone, so he could study the young woman sitting out on the deck of the small houseboat moored next to his yacht. He had seen her storm out and make the crude gesture towards his yacht just after the fireworks had finished, and it had amused him greatly.

Not only that, but the girl was achingly beautiful: bi-racial, he guessed; Asian; her almond eyes; the olive skin; the dark hair tumbling around her shoulders—an exquisite face even in anger.

It had been a while since Raziel Ganz had been surprised by a woman. The ladies that he attracted knew of his wealth and tried to land him as a partner, a future husband, but he wasn't interested in commitment—not with those women. Where was the challenge, the fire, the excitement?

No. He'd much rather spar with the young woman who owned that damn ramshackle houseboat. She was clearly unimpressed by wealth, and that was thrilling to him.

At forty-four, Raziel Ganz presented an aura of corporate wealth, ruthless business acumen, and dazzling good looks to the world, and he enjoyed everything that brought him. He slept around, yes, but rarely called any of the woman back—no, scratch that—he *never* called *any* woman back.

This woman, though, might prove interesting. She would certainly look good on his arm when he met Satchel Rose, his mark for this visit to Portland. Rose was notoriously private—elusive *and* reclusive—and the fact he'd agreed to a meeting with Raziel was a major victory. If Raziel wanted to move some of his shipping corporation to Portland, he would have to have Rose on side to secure the city's welcome.

And Rose would give him the air of authenticity that he needed to cover his real business...

For now though, Raziel lit a cigarette and watched the beauty on the houseboat. She seemed to sense his scrutiny and glared up in his direction. As he watched, amused, she again threw a middle finger up, got up, and stalked back into her home, slamming the door behind her.

Raz smiled. *Yes.* She would be his kind of challenge.

CHAPTER TWO

"You look like crap."

Winter half-grinned at her student and her friend. "Always such a silver-tongued devil. Thank you."

Joseph Matts, his hair coaxed up into a Mohican, shrugged. "Sorry, boo, but it's unusual for you to look bad, so it's more noticeable." He checked himself. Joseph was bipolar and sometimes spoke his mind without thinking. "Sorry. I meant that as a compliment."

Winter's smile was wide now. "I know, honey." She rubbed his back. Joe was one of the few people she could stand to be around, which was why she considered him her friend as well as a paying student.

Joe was around her age, maybe even a little older, and was a sensational musician. He was way past what Winter would consider as needing lessons, but the truth was, she knew Joe felt comfortable with her, and she helped him write songs for his two-man band. Joe's wife, Cassie, was also a friend; she and Joe so in love that it made Winter's heart ache. Cassie kept Joe steady, managing his medication and his moods with an expert touch. Winter always told her she had the looks of a cheerleader and the brain of a Nobel Prize winner.

Cassie was a sweetheart even if she did tend to 'mother' Winter a little. Winter didn't mind that so much.

Joe sat down at the piano as Winter grabbed her folder. "What were we doing last time?"

"New song. The one about darkness."

"They're *all* about darkness," Winter shot back with a laugh. "We're the cheerful twins, remember?"

"Word." Joe grinned at her. "You know, I was talking to Josh… we could always use a third member."

"Ha, thanks, but no thanks. I'm not a performer. Not anymore."

She was interrupted by a knock on the door of her houseboat. Winter and Joe frowned at each other. She never got unplanned visitors. Winter got up and went to the door. A smiling delivery man greeted her and handed her a huge hamper. "Courtesy of Mr. Ganz. An apology for the inconvenience of his party last night."

Before Winter could react, the man had gone. She staggered back inside with the heavy hamper and dumped it on her couch.

"What the hell?" Joseph was up, looking curious. Winter sighed.

"Dude in the big yacht next door trying to buy my forgiveness for keeping me awake all night. Which is why I look like crap, by the way. I can't keep this."

Joe held his hands up, grinning. "Woah, woah! Wait until you check out what's inside."

"Joe."

"I'm serious. Come on, open up."

Sighing, Winter opened up the hamper reluctantly, sincerely wanting to just reject it immediately.

"Damn." Joseph whistled, and Winter gaped at what was inside: Champagne, caviar, truffles, and a myriad of artisanal cold cuts, cheeses, and other luxury foods. Joe plucked the card from the hamper. "Read! Read!"

Winter snatched it from him, grinning. "Damn, boy, you are so nosy." She opened it and read aloud what it said. "Please accept my apologies for the disturbance last night, dear lady. I hope this goes some way to making up for it. Perhaps you would like to join me for drinks tonight? Raziel Ganz." She rolled her eyes. "*Dear lady*?"

Joe snorted. "Perhaps he and Mr. Darcy teamed up to write that card. How does he know he upset you?"

Winter grinned. "I gave him the bird. Twice. He might not have seen the first time, but he definitely saw the second time." She felt pleased that her nemesis had seen her anger. She looked down at the hamper. It had to be said, this food would be a welcome asset to her bare cupboards—she'd been living on ramen and pasta for the last week or so. Joe was watching her carefully.

"Win? There would be nothing wrong with keeping this, you know? You wouldn't owe him anything but a polite thank you."

Winter flushed. Joe was one of the few people who knew she struggled to make ends meet—he and Cassie often invited Winter over to eat with them, and Cassie always managed to send Winter home with the leftovers. Winter wished she didn't need to take their kind charity, but a girl needed to eat. She paid them back by working with Joe for his songwriting and not charging for the extra time. It made her feel as if she were giving something back at least. "It's a lot."

"Well, he kept you awake, and I know how you feel about fireworks…"

Winter nodded. "Yup." She grinned ruefully. "I have to admit, that ham looks amazing."

"It does, and you know what, that reminds me… Cassie and I would love to have you over for Thanksgiving… if you're not with your family, of course."

Winter's heart sank. "No. I won't be with them." Not for a couple of years now, and she couldn't see a time when she would be again.

Joe rubbed her shoulder. "Then it's decided."

She smiled at him. He may look like a punk rocker who didn't give a crap, but Joe really was the sweetest guy she had ever known. He felt like family to her now as did Cassie; Joe was the brother Winter had never had. "If you're sure?"

"Very. Now, should we get on?"

Winter nodded, closing the hamper and leaving the card on top. She'd decide what to do about it later. "We should. Let's get to it."

Raziel had smiled to himself when he saw the delivery guy turn up at the girl's houseboat with the hamper. He watched as surprise registered on her lovely face, then a stiff nod. She wasn't someone who took charity, he could see that.

And now he knew her name as well. Winter Mai. His private investigator had taken less than an hour to find about her. Twenty-seven and a piano tutor. Living alone. No family in the Portland area. Survived the mall shooting massacre in Seattle a few years back, but was seriously injured.

Ah. Raz suddenly understood the reason for her anger last night. *The fireworks. Damn.* Well, at least he could apologize for that and cancel his plans for any further shows. It was the least he could do. His private investigator had turned up some photos of her, too. Christ, she was stunning. Dark brown eyes, olive skin, long dark hair with burnished mahogany highlights. A petite curvy body: soft, sensual. His gaze lingered over that exquisite face and that pink rosebud mouth—so inviting, so kissable.

Yes. She would be a challenge, but he was confident he could seduce her. *Good.* He was bored with the usual suspects when it came to his bed partners. He wondered how long she would hold out before she succumbed to his charms... it wouldn't be long.

He turned as his personal assistant, Gareth, knocked at his office door and came in. "Hey, boss."

"Gareth. What's on for today?"

"Unfortunately there's still no confirmation from the Satchel Rose camp on when he'll meet with you, but I do have intel he'll be at a function for the Portland Public Library in a couple of weeks."

Raz's eyebrows shot up. "Rose? Out in public?"

Gareth smiled. "Seems he has ties to the library—family ties, I think. Not quite sure in what manner."

"Find out, would you? And call the library. Tell them I'd like to attend."

"Sure thing."

When he was alone, Raziel's thoughts turned back to the beautiful young woman on the houseboat. He would go see her personally this afternoon to give her little room to reject him.

Winter Mai would be the perfect date for the library benefit and to meet Satchel Rose, and he, Raziel, always got what he wanted.

Always.

CHAPTER THREE

Satchel Rose sighed as someone knocked at his study door. He'd hoped not to be interrupted for the morning, so he could indulge in his favorite task: designing buildings. He'd gotten a couple of hours of drawing and planning done, but now his assistant was interrupting his flow, and he knew he wouldn't get it back again. "Come in."

Molly stuck her head around the door, an apologetic expression on her sweet face. "I'm sorry, Satch. I wouldn't interrupt, but your father called again. Wanted to get your yes or no for Thanksgiving, and he insisted I come ask you. I think he's worried you won't turn up and referee."

Satchel smiled despite himself. His father, Patrick, was a loving but weak-willed man who was terrified of his new wife, Janelle. Satchel, on the other hand, *adored* Janelle, although he jokingly called her his step-monster. The African-American college professor gave as good as she got, teasing Satchel mercilessly, and also ruling her husband's life, challenging him, egging him on, not letting him rest on his laurels in his retirement. They'd been together for twenty years but had only recently tied the knot.

Satchel smiled at Molly now. "I'll call the house, Mols. Thanks."

"No problem, boss."

Satchel called the house; both his father and Janelle refused to get cellphones, which Satchel found cute and annoying in equal measure. Janelle answered his call.

"Hey, Brat."

"Hey, Monster. I have been summoned."

Janelle laughed, her giggle mischievous. "Your dad is crapping his pants. I told him all my sisters and my mom are coming to Thanksgiving. It's not true, of course, but he's convinced he'll be outnumbered."

Satchel laughed loudly. "You really are *evil*. I love it."

"Here's your dad. Don't rat me out..." she whispered before raising her voice slightly. Satchel's dad was a little deaf. "Your son, or so he says. I think he's actually the spawn of the devil." She cackled with laughter, then her voice grew fond as she spoke to Satchel again. "Just kidding. Love you, Brat. Bye, sweetie."

"Bye, gorgeous. Love you, too." Satchel waited until his dad took the phone and said hello. "Hey, Pa, how are you doing?"

"*Women*." Patrick said with a quiver in his voice. "There's going to be women everywhere. She has six sisters, Satch! *Six!*"

Satchel grinned to himself. "Pa, most men would be grateful to be surrounded by women."

"Six sisters, Satchel. *Six. And* the mother."

"You love Janelle's family, come on."

Patrick harrumphed. "I love them... from a distance. Just promise me you'll be there."

"I promise, Pa. Calm down."

That seemed to settle his father. "Bringing anyone? How about that Molly? She's a sweetheart; I don't know why you haven't snapped her up."

"Because, Pa, I possess something that she isn't the least bit interested in."

"What could that possibly be, son?"

Satchel grinned. "A penis, Pa. I've told you before. Molly is very happily married to a wonderful woman."

More grumbling and muttering from his father, and Satchel laughed. "Pa, look, there's no one at the moment, and I'm fine with that."

"There hasn't been for a couple of years, Satch. I'm worried."

"Pa... come on. I'm too old for you to be worrying about that." Satchel swallowed the irritation that always bubbled up when his dad fretted about his son's lack of love life. "I'm fussy, and I like my own space."

"Hermit."

"Yup, unashamedly so."

There was a short silence on the end of the line. "As long as you're not still blaming yourself for... you know."

Satchel's chest felt tight. "No, Pa." A lie—and they both knew it. "Look, I have to go. I'll be at Thanksgiving, I promise."

"Good. Love you, son."

"Love you, too, Pa."

He hung up and rubbed his face as he headed to the small executive bathroom next to his office. Satchel worked from home as much as possible, but even his home was set out like an office, with Molly having her own private space in which to work. She was about the only person he could stand to be around for long periods, but even then, sometimes he felt the overwhelming need to be alone. Luckily, Molly seemed to sense when he was going through one of his hermit phases and would leave him alone as much as she could, running interference on people who wanted more time than Satchel was willing to give.

Satchel splashed water on his face and studied his reflection. At almost forty, he knew he had aged into a handsome man, but his looks were a hindrance as far as Satchel was concerned. Dark hair, swarthy skin from his late Italian mother, and bright green eyes were like catnip to both women and men. When he had been younger, he had been a beautiful boy and had made the most of it:

sleeping around, enjoying life. Being sociable. When had that changed?

You know when, he told himself. He closed his eyes, scrunching them up. God, when he would he just get over it? *It wasn't your fault Callan Flint went crazy with that gun. It wasn't your responsibility to 'save' him.*

So why did he feel like it was? Ever since the St Anne's Mall massacre, Satchel had felt himself withdrawing from public life. Callan had been his best friend, and he hadn't noticed how bad things had gotten.

No one had, but Satchel was the person closest to Callan, and even he hadn't seen it. Twenty-seven people dead. Fifty three injured. Satchel had paid for every funeral and all the medical expenses and had to be stopped from giving away all of his money to the survivors. Callan's parents had stepped in then. "Satchel, this isn't your fault. We need to do something, too—make reparations."

And so, the Flint family had paid out compensation to the victims. It wasn't like they couldn't afford it—both the Rose and Flint families were billionaires several times over. But for Satchel, it didn't feel as he'd done enough. He became increasingly despondent and only found peace when he was alone.

He pushed those thoughts aside for now, knowing they would return as they always did to routinely haunt his days. To distract himself, he powered on the television and flicked through the channels. He stopped when he came to a food and cooking channel, his attention caught by the woman presenting. Autumn Mai. He knew that name all too well. The Mai family. Three sisters, Autumn, Summer, and Winter. Autumn was the only one of them left physically unscathed by the shooting. Summer had been killed by a single bullet to her throat. Winter, the youngest, had been the worst of the injured, shot six times in the chest and stomach at point-blank range and not expected to live.

Satchel, unbeknownst to everyone, had often sat by the young woman's bed late at night, after visiting hours. It was time his money could buy. He didn't know her at all and hadn't spoken to her family, but there was something so vulnerable about her. Christ, she was just a kid.

Then, without warning, one day her family secretly transferred her to a different hospital, and he lost track of her. It felt like a death. He'd been channeling all his guilt into this one victim, and when she was removed from his life, his guilt had nowhere to go but internally.

He watched her older sister now, Autumn. A celebrity chef even before the shooting, she was confident and affable on screen and obviously loved her chosen profession. A stunningly beautiful woman, her Asian parentage obvious in her features and her dark hair piled up on her head as she moved gracefully around the set.

Satchel sighed. Maybe he could get past the guilt if he found out where Autumn's sister had gone. If he could see her, apologize to her in person...

But that would be an incredible invasion of privacy and selfish of him, too. No, he had to face his demons on his own.

He just didn't know where the hell to start.

End of Sneak Peek.

Start Reading Dangerous Desire NOW!

https://books2read.com/u/bOAL7Q

©Copyright 2022 by Michelle Love - All rights Reserved

In no way is it legal to reproduce, duplicate, or transmit any part of this document in either electronic means or in printed format.

Recording of this publication is strictly prohibited, and any storage of this document is not allowed unless with written permission from the publisher.

All rights are reserved.

Respective authors own all copyrights not held by the publisher.

❀ Created with Vellum